DOCTOR SLAUGHTER

By the same author

Fiction
Waldo
Fong and the Indians
Murder in Mount Holly
Girls at Play
Jungle Lovers
Sinning with Annie
Saint Jack
The Black House
The Family Arsenal
The Consul's File
Picture Palace
A Christmas Card
London Snow
World's End
The Mosquito Coast
The London Embassy

Criticism
V. S. Naipaul

Non-fiction
The Great Railway Bazaar
The Old Patagonian Express
The Kingdom by the Sea

WITHDRAWN FROM
THE LIBRARY

UNIVERSITY OF
WINCHESTER

KING ALFRED'S COLLEGE
WINCHESTER

To be returned on or before the day marked below :—

23. NOV. 1995

PLEASE ENTER ON ISSUE SLIP:

AUTHOR THEROUX

TITLE Doctor Slaughter

ACCESSION No. 3046

KA 0033188 0

Doctor Slaughter

PAUL THEROUX

HAMISH HAMILTON

London

KING ALFRED'S COLLEGE
WINCHESTER

813.<u>54</u>
THE 3046

First published in Great Britain 1984
by Hamish Hamilton Ltd
Garden House 57–59 Long Acre London WC2E 9JZ

Copyright © 1984 by Paul Theroux·

British Library Cataloguing in Publication Data

Theroux, Paul
  Doctor Slaughter.
  I. Title
  813'.54[F]   PS3570.H4
  ISBN 0-241-11255-9

Typeset by Rowland Phototypesetting Ltd
Printed in Great Britain by
St Edmundsbury Press Ltd, Bury St Edmunds, Suffolk

For Gillon Aitken

1

At first Lauren had liked being new to London and not knowing a soul. Being a stranger was a thrill, like being in disguise – full of those possibilities. And she believed that strangers were among the few people in the world who could be trusted with the truth. She loved telling them her secrets, and discovering theirs. But the city, so far, had disappointed her: London wasn't London. She had not seen anything here that she had expected, and after a month she had seen too much that she had never expected.

This morning she was standing in her freezing room, wearing her mink-lined coat, thinking about the General's dinner party – the incredible thing the guest had said.

'There are five thousand people in the world.' And he had smiled at those on the left of the table, then – taking his time – those on the right. Finally, his eyes came to rest on the woman who had been saying 'absolutely' all evening. She did not say 'absolutely' now.

The people at the table offered one of those silences that was intended to let the man finish. It had certainly seemed like an unfinished sentence. But the man just smiled again and lifted his knife and worked it through the fist of meat bleeding on his plate.

She had found out his name during the first course. Taking her fork out of her mousseline she had pointed it at the wall just behind the General.

[1]

'That painting looks like a Van Goh,' she said.

'Van Goff,' the General said.

'Fon Hokh,' the man said, and then, 'I should know that, as a Van Arkady.'

He had done more talking than the host. At these London dinner parties the host often seemed the least important or the quietest person in the room. The host was interesting only because he brought much more interesting people together – so it seemed to Lauren. General Sir George Newhouse, head of the Hemisphere Institute, was famous for his guests and famous for saying very little. He had only opened his mouth once tonight and that was to mispronounce the name of the Dutch painter. But it had hardly been noticed, for Van Arkady was still talking. They were now on the main course.

He said, 'That's it. The population of the world. Five thousand.'

They had been discussing recent catastrophes – the scale of them in human lives: almost a million dead in the Ethiopian famine, half a million refugees in Lebanon, ten thousand throats cut in a massacre in India, and the most recent Chinese earthquake upwards of two million either dead or homeless.

The Chinese statistic was Lauren's, and when she said it (someone whispered, 'I had no idea there was an earthquake there last year!'), Van Arkady stammered for attention and then delivered his pronouncement about there being five thousand people in the world.

It sank in – he meant just that. It was a very London way of speaking – abrupt and cynical and knowing, like a polite way of starting trouble. Lauren had once asked General Newhouse about a certain Arabic scholar and the General shrugged and said, 'He doesn't exist.' And when you cut someone at a party, she had been told, it was not that you were ignoring the person or that you were turning away – it was that the person was not there: you saw nothing. It was all a London manner she was trying to get used to.

Everyone turned to her when Lauren said, 'China's population has officially reached one billion.'

'That's official,' Van Arkady said. 'I am speaking of reality.'

'Yes, in reality there are a billion people in China.'

'Wrong,' he said. 'There are two people in China.' He was smiling at Lauren. 'I know both of them.'

'I never touch salt,' Lauren said to the man next to her who was offering her a little hopper of salt with a tiny spoon stuck in it. 'But if I did, I certainly wouldn't spoon it out of that thing.' Then her face became radiant and she smiled at Van Arkady. 'Two people in China. I love it.'

'I've been to China,' Van Arkady said.

'Everyone's been to China,' Lauren said, still smiling.

Lady Newhouse said, 'Hugo, did it ever occur to you that you might not be one of those five thousand?'

'The thought never entered my head,' Van Arkady said.

Lauren at that moment seriously wondered: If he's right, am I one of them? It did not come in words. She saw herself fleetingly in half shadow as a small dim rejected figure without a face. She worried for a few uncertain seconds that Van Arkady might be joking. He had talked the whole time, acting as host – pouring wine and pronouncing. Who was he?

The others had become nervous; the conversation had

[3]

faltered. She hoped it was not a joke. She could not see a joke in it. It was so extraordinary she wanted it to be true.

'And I have a theory,' Van Arkady said – and people relaxed a little, glad that he was managing all the talk; he was ugly and interesting, about her father's age, but dark; and what sort of name was Van Arkady? 'This theory is that if you live long enough you meet them all.'

'It's a metaphor!' Julian Shuttle said – too loud, he was very angry and speaking to the table at large. He was young, about Lauren's age, and had recently been asked by General Newhouse to join the Hemisphere Institute. When Lauren told the General that she had decided not to study China, as she had planned, but to start from scratch on the Persian Gulf, she was put in Julian's office. Julian was an Arabist. Lauren suspected that the General was trying to frighten her into resuming her studies of the Chinese economy. But Julian was not the sort to intimidate her, and when she said that she didn't know anything about the Gulf he said, 'Don't worry about it. That's what fellowships are for.' He was kind and intelligent, and although he was Lauren's age he had an endearing way of behaving like her younger brother.

'A metaphor?' Van Arkady said. 'No, it is not that at all.' His manner was patronizing. He did not insist and it made him seem very sure of himself. 'It is a fact. I can name many of them.'

'Carry on,' Julian said, looking nervous and bold.

Van Arkady said, 'The names would mean nothing to you, young man.'

Lauren admired the man's roosterish arrogance. When she was impressed her face shone, the excitement whipped up her blood and made her prettier. And the man's arrogance somehow went with his ugliness and made him majestic.

'What about the rest of the people in the world?' Julian asked. His voice cracked a little – he was upset, and he seemed beseeching rather than challenging.

Van Arkady ignored Julian. He turned to the other dinner guests. But he answered Julian's question. He said, 'The rest don't really matter. A million dead here, two million there – it is part of a natural cycle. Yes, even massacres. There is murder in nature. Please don't think I'm insensitive. I believe the death of one man can change the course of history, when it is the right man and when we are fully conscious of it. But a million don't matter, because it isn't a number in any actual sense, unless it is applied to money. A million dollars is an easy thing, but a million men is impossible to imagine. My five thousand is reality, but' – and here he smiled at Julian Shuttle – 'a million men is a metaphor.'

Julian seemed to sulk at this, and at the end of the table Mrs Timothy Beach whispered, 'My cleaning lady said, "A blue foulard – that's a kind of duck, isn't it?" '

'We don't feel a million,' Van Arkady was saying. 'You can't honestly say that you miss all those Ethiopians and Chinese. Their deaths don't change anything, and a truthful but callous person might argue that we're all a jolly sight better off without them. We make a pointless virtue out of keeping people alive. It is one of the follies of our century – it is a mere conceit, making us feel powerful. But it is sometimes much kinder to allow people to die in their own way than to keep them alive our way.'

Lauren was thrilled at this – not the details of the argument

[5]

but the calm cruel way the man stated it, and she wanted him to notice her approval.

Over dessert it became a game. How many of the five thousand were British or German or African? Van Arkady considered each question seriously and answered 'Forty-five' and 'Sixty' and 'None.'

He said, 'And more Arabs than you might think.'

'I do Arabs,' Lauren said.

'The ones I am speaking of are all here in London.'

'In other words, no Bedouin,' Lady Newhouse said.

'What is a Bedouin?' Mrs Beach asked.

Lauren said, 'They're people who like to live in tents.'

The man on Lauren's left – Giles something, from the Foreign Office – said, 'Aren't you going to eat your syllabub?'

'Is that what it's called?' Lauren said, and she laughed out loud. Then she said, 'No, I kind of watch my sugar-intake.'

'And you didn't touch your duckling.'

'I don't eat meat,' she said.

'Did you know Hitler was a vegetarian?' he said, and he scowled and made his eyebrows devilish. Then he relented. 'So was George Bernard Shaw.'

Lauren said, 'I've never read him.'

'You've missed something,' the man said.

'No. I'll never read him. I think it's very unlucky to read Shaw's books. My uncle was reading a book by him when he died.'

Lady Newhouse stood up and said, 'Anyone who would like to freshen up –'

'I'm going to miss you,' the man said.

'I'm not going anywhere,' Lauren said.

'You're being summoned,' he said. 'Ladies to the loo, while the men pass the port and cigars around.'

'What a nerve,' Lauren said softly. 'And this is a black-tie dinner.'

'The General is very old-fashioned.'

'To me that always means a complete asshole.'

The man began to stifle a laugh, and then he gave in to it and said, 'But you don't drink!'

'You notice everything,' Lauren said. 'Anyway, it's the principle I object to.'

'Or do you want a cigar?' He had taken two thick cigars out of a leather wallet and he held one under her chin.

'Where I come from,' she said, 'we call that a sour dick.'

She was taken to a narrow parlour-like room with the five other women and they took turns using the adjoining toilet. One by one, they spent far too long behind the door and returned with different faces – like masks made of pastry flour and food colouring: the first time Lauren heard the word 'tarts' she thought of the glazed and frosted faces of these old women.

But one wore no make-up. She was a frog-faced woman who wobbled in her shoes and when she took her turn in the toilet the other women exchanged glances. Lauren suspected it was Van Arkady's wife.

'Five thousand people,' one woman said, mocking the man by making his accent seem foreign.

'He is so full of himself,' Mrs Beach said.

Then Lauren was sure that the frog-faced woman was Mrs Van Arkady.

'Ginnie,' Lady Newhouse cautioned.

[7]

But Mrs Beach, who was seated in a chair next to Lauren, was still talking in a low defiant voice.

'He's a fornicator,' she said.

Lauren laughed, and when she saw Van Arkady again in the Newhouses' drawing-room – they were having coffee – she wanted to go home with him. His ugly wife was a burden to him – she looked unhealthy and bad-tempered. She certainly wasn't one of the five thousand!

'What do you do?' Lauren said to Van Arkady.

The question surprised him, but he looked pleased and said, 'I'm just one of these boring bankers.'

Lauren said, 'I find money incredibly exciting.'

'I sometimes think that money has no existence,' Van Arkady said. 'It is simply something that certain people believe in – and they have given it a kind of temporary reality. It is a bubble – it must be, because in the past it has actually burst. And of course that will happen again.'

He was edging sideways as he spoke, moving Lauren towards the fireplace, where logs were flaming – she could feel the heat against her legs.

'And what is your profession?' Van Arkady said.

She said, 'I do just about everything.'

'Surely not everything,' he said, dropping his voice.

'When I feel like it,' Lauren said lightly.

Just then, Mrs Van Arkady – small, sallow, with shins like knifeblades and wearing big blue shoes – stepped over and claimed her husband, who was still smiling and a little breathless from the way Lauren had seemed to dare him.

But men were so slow, and she felt she always had to do all

the work and make it easy for them, and then she had to seem surprised when they at last made a move.

She watched the Van Arkadys go to the foyer, and to be persistent – to show herself again – she went downstairs after them and found her own coat, and waited to be asked whether she needed a lift. But the ugly woman had probably said something to her husband, because he looked a little sheepish and only said, 'What a wonderful coat,' and helped her on with it. She wanted to face him and say that she believed that she was one of the five thousand he had spoken of.

But instead she said, 'Thanks' and let her gaze linger on him. He was a cruel and henpecked man – but just like her father, and like many men, who were savage and brilliant in company, but at home they wore aprons and called their wives 'Queenie' and got furious trying to be helpful.

Lauren saw herself as he must have seen her – standing in her warm coat under the crystal chandelier in the General's foyer in Eaton Row. Her hair was shining and her skin was clear and she was six feet tall in these shoes; she saw herself as pretty and powerful, and she was sure he regarded her as smart and well-off and that he wanted to know her and to get rid of his awful wife. She imagined saying, 'We'll turn heads' and saw herself entering The Ritz with him. Why were men so slow?

Women hate me, Lauren thought, sensing Mrs Van Arkady's poisonous eyes on her. She believed that other women always envied and disliked her and saw her as a threat – it was one of her many satisfactions.

She knew she had left an impression on Van Arkady – she could see it in the General's mirrors – it was the perfect house to be seen in. But she left alone and walked to Victoria Station and took the tube back to her bedsitter. Tube was the perfect name for it at this time of night, and when she got back to her horrible room she discovered her toilet was frozen solid. London!

2

The mink-lined coat was her own idea. 'My own design,' she said. But it was a simple design: a good plain Burberry with a fur lining – twenty-seven mink pelts that were hidden when the coat was buttoned up. It was the warmest coat she had ever owned.

Women who wore minks were show-offs, like her mother, who hadn't even needed it in Virginia. This mink lining had once been her mother's whole coat. A second-hand mink was a pardonable thing, but a new one was a crime. A black tailor named Noosie had carefully cut the old thing and fitted it into the new Burberry. Lauren did not pay the tailor, but later the sixty-two-year-old man took her to dinner – she regarded her agreeing to go as a kind of payment – and afterwards in his room she allowed him to take photographs of her neck, from the front. That was Noosie's odd request. 'More neck, darling,' he kept saying.

She unfastened the top buttons of her blouse and sat straighter. She thought: Necko-philia! She wanted to laugh.

But he was very solemn; he was perspiring. His black face was beady-wet like a cold plum. He shot two rolls of film, stepping in a circle around her.

If he wants it I'll go the whole nine yards, Lauren thought. But when he was out of film he made her a cup of cocoa and walked her to the bus stop. She had prepared herself for something else, because she had wanted this useful two-sided coat.

She needed it in this freezing room. She hated the place, and she thought how unfair it was that she should go unrecognized. No one had yet seen how special she was: pretty, healthy, intelligent, well-travelled – and she had style. She had no money – that was a bitch – but money was never hard to find. Yet brains and beauty and health! Did those women last night have any idea how foolish and empty they were, how ugly and neurotic, with a cigarette in one claw and a drink in the other? They coughed like outboard motors!

They hated her because she was young and, somehow, they knew she had been to China and was planning a trip to the Middle East. She could run a fast five miles, she was the first American woman Fellow at the Institute, she had once made love to her art history professor's wife. 'I'm eclectic,' she said. She had represented Culpeper at the Miss Virginia pageant in the State Fair. The professor's wife was an impulse – she had invited Lauren for coffee and touched her hair. Lauren had looked calmly into her eyes and seen a harmless lust, and she said what the woman was too afraid to say: 'I want to scarf you,' and did, there on the sofa, with the woman's dress pushed up around her waist and the woman tipped back and whimpering a little, as if she was giving birth. Lauren counted that afternoon as one of her accomplishments, because she was not sorry and she had not repeated it.

She did not deserve this Brixton bedsitter. It was heated by a small electric fire – two bars on a tin plate fixed to the sealed-up hearth, but it was unsafe and expensive to leave it burning. The day before she had stayed at the Institute and gone straight to the party and in those eighte n hours the toilet in the small cubicle in the hall had frozen. There was still ice in it now and frost on the black windows. London dampness was colder than any ice she had ever seen, and London ice was like dark stone – a kind of dirty swelling marble. Seeing the toilet she had said to herself, as if to a friend, 'And I looked down and saw there was actually ice in the john!'

But she knew she would never tell anyone, which was a shame, because even though it was disgusting it was also very funny. It made a good story, but she knew she would have to be a success before she could tell it, otherwise she would be pitied.

Still in her mink coat she went into the hallway, where there was a pay phone. She found a likely number in the phone book and stood in her warm coat, dialling, and when Lindsay from upstairs passed by her and said, 'All right?' she was pleased with herself, because underneath her coat she had nothing on, and he didn't know it. She enjoyed her terrific secret – standing there naked inside her coat.

'I'd like to speak to the plumber,' she said, when the call went through. Even on the phone she took pleasure in the half truth of being naked inside her coat.

'Yeah, this is the plumber.'

She was oddly encouraged by the stupid selfish tone of the man.

'The most incredible thing happened last night,' she said, and took a breath. 'My toilet turned to ice! I don't know what to do. I mean, what good is a frozen toilet?'

'You American?'

'I sure am   she said.

'I can't do anything before tomorrow,' he said in a slightly friendlier tone.

'What about this evening,' she said, 'around Happy Hour – or whatever you people call cocktail time?'

He fell silent, but then he asked for her address and she knew he would come that evening.

'Coldharbour Lane,' he said. 'That's Brixton.'

'Brixton is my new home,' she said.

'What do you think of it?'

'Come on over and I'll tell you.'

'Name?'

'Lauren Slaughter.'

*

Even that – her name – was half true. The gold initials on her briefcase said *L.S.* because it had been her husband's. Leonard Slaughter was English, and very serious. He taught economics at Hull. Hull was horrible! They had met in China and married in Washington and had separated in London. They had China in common, and after they parted she saw his close-set eyes and big serious nose whenever she heard the word China. And anything Chinese stirred memories of her marriage. It was this that influenced her in wanting to change her field of study to the Arab world.

Leonard had not wanted a divorce, but it was pointless to live the way they had been living, making a virtue of merely holding on. Leonard cared about appearances, which made him tenacious. Marriage was not a virtuous thing, only a balancing act, two people pedalling a tandem bike, one behind the other, the man in front. It was absurd and pleasant like that, and just as rare a success as in life – no, it was a short-distance thing and he steered and she pedalled. All marriage had done for her was give her a new name. Her old one was Mopsy Fairlight. She took the name Lauren when she got the name Slaughter. She wondered why people didn't change their names more often. She laughed and then concentrated hard when she saw her old name written on the flyleaf of some of her books – the words, the ink, the signature: where was this girl now?

Last night's dinner party had left her feeling rumpled and dissatisfied, as if she had been stupidly teased. In this mood she went to work. On the Victoria Line to Green Park and the Institute she repeated her sentence 'When I feel like it' and she was pleased by the way it sounded. She liked her reflection in the train window. She was a young woman with a girl's face – the features almost of a child – but she was stronger than most men she knew; she could run faster and farther than they. Jogging at a certain speed, Leonard had always looked as if he was just going to fly apart.

At Stockwell a man got on and sat across the aisle from Lauren. He was a television director, or else an actor, or something in advertising. He was wearing lovely shoes – olive green, probably Italian – and he had nice narrow feet. He also wore a felt hat, innocently gangsterish. A young man who wore that kind of hat wanted to call attention to himself. He was dressed warmly – a Crombie overcoat with soft sleeves, and blue jeans. He was trying to look interesting and self-absorbed and he sat there comfortably with his *Guardian* still

folded on his lap unread. Lauren found him sexy and self-
assured – but for her they were almost the same thing.
Something in his clothes and his manner suggested that he
had been to the States. This she found attractive in him. She
hated the house-bound English.

She was peering past him, seeming to ignore him. But it
was not shyness or lack of interest – she was looking at his
reflection in the window and she wanted to give him a chance
to look at her.

Then she made her move. She reached into her briefcase
and took out *Renmin Ribao* – it was two months old, but how
could he tell? She held it up and began reading busily.

'You read –' He smiled and pointed.

She smiled back at him over the top of the paper. 'Chinese.'

He had been quicker than most – seconds – but in that time
she had actually found an article she had missed on other
readings, and it was related to her new area – something
about a Chinese trade delegation to the Persian Gulf. The
Chinese were in the oil business, too, and had machinery to
sell – this she gathered while the man waited for her to say
something more.

He was not handsome but stylish – worldly, unattached,
definitely not serious. He looked fun. He was something in
television, she was sure.

Lauren folded the Chinese newspaper in half and held it
out to him.

'Want to do the crossword?'

He laughed, but took the paper and examined it and
remarked what an amazing language it was. 'You must be very
clever.'

[16]

She said, 'On the other hand, I don't speak French and you probably do.'

'You speak American,' he said.

'Don't be cruel,' she said, and tenderly touched his arm.

The train was drawing into Victoria.

'I hate this stop,' she said. 'All the commuters.'

He shrugged and said, 'I'm not going far.'

She wanted to know how far, how long she would have with him, but instead of asking she made an amused face to show that she had not understood what he had just said.

'Oxford Circus,' he said, in explanation.

'I'll join you.'

He said he was a film editor for Olympus Pictures and that he had lived in the States for a year – New York. He then said, 'Do you get back often?'

'Periodically.'

He stared at her and repeated 'periodically' – trying it out.

'You should go to Virginia sometime,' she said. 'But there's no point going unless you have me to show you around.'

He did not say anything in reply. He waited until the train drew into Oxford Circus and then, when the platform was clear, he said, 'I'll keep that in mind. In the meantime, maybe we could discuss it over dinner.'

The serious ones always said dinner. She had not expected this from him. His seriousness slightly oppressed her. They walked upstairs. She did not tell him that she had missed her stop for him.

'My name's Lauren.'

'Ivan Shepherd.'

At the top of the stairs she took a card out of her wallet. She

[17]

liked handing over her printed card, with her new name and the two phone numbers and the Institute's embossed hemisphere – the world in gold. It was a ritual that made her feel important and protected.

'The Hemisphere Institute of International Studies,' he said, reading from the card. He had no expression, he was thinking hard; he said, 'You went past your stop.'

'I have shopping to do,' she said, and turned quickly and walked away while he was still gaping at her. And once she was out of sight she ran all the way to the Institute.

There was a seminar that morning on tensions in the Gulf. It was always tensions somewhere – the world was a wreck. This one concerned the war between Iran and Iraq, its effect on the Shatt-al-Arab waterway, but it was being held at London University over in Russell Square. Instead of going, Lauren spent the morning in the Institute library – an irritating morning, as it turned out, because the librarian would not allow her to use the photocopying machine.

'This is for staff use only,' the woman said. 'There's a coin-operated one on the third floor for the use of Institute Fellows.'

Lauren said that Mr Fletcher always let her use this machine.

The librarian said, 'Then Mr Fletcher is breaking the rules.'

Mr Fletcher was a lovely nervous little guy who lived with his mother; but this librarian was an insensitive woman with a chafed face and old brown shoes.

*

Julian returned from the seminar at one. When he was overworked he looked like an old man – round-shouldered and preoccupied and harmless.

'How about lunch?' Lauren said. 'It's on me.'

In the coffee shop on the south side of Berkeley Square, Julian said that the party had made him furious. He had spent the whole night wakeful, thinking angrily about the man who had said, 'There are five thousand people in the world.'

Lauren thought it was one of the brightest things she had heard in London so far – unless the man had been joking: she was still a little uneasy about that.

Julian said, 'I wish I had said something scathing to him. I hate these people who are full of formulas and magic numbers.'

'He was pretty incredible,' Lauren said.

'He's a monster.'

Lauren did not want to be drawn into a discussion of the man at the dinner – she was uncomfortable talking about things she wanted or people she liked.

'So how was the seminar?' she said.

Julian said that it had been poorly attended, and so they had been able to put a lot of questions to the people who had read papers. He described how the Arabs in the marshes of southern Iraq had been driven away, and their unique settlements which had lasted for thousands of years in this remote place were now destroyed by two trampling armies. The economy of Kuwait had been affected by the war, too. A man at the seminar named Haseeb was organizing a study tour of the Gulf.

'I'd love to go,' Lauren said.

'You should have been at the seminar.'

'I couldn't be bothered to go all the way to Bloomsbury.'

'You're astonishing,' he said, and looked Lauren over admiringly. 'That's a splendid coat.'

'I designed it,' she said. 'I design all my own dresses.'

'My sister does that.'

Lauren was irritated by his saying this. She said, 'But I design everything. I'd design my own underwear, too, if I wore any, except I don't.'

Julian seemed both shocked and grateful.

'I don't buy knickers,' she said, playfully pursing her lips on the word. 'Why do English people like that word so much?'

Julian said, 'Because we're pathetic and repressed.'

Lauren was pinching her empty purse and fussing with it, but before she could say, 'I left all my money at the Institute' Julian said, 'My treat' and insisted that lunch had been his idea, not hers.

'I hope you don't think I'm as coarse as this with everyone,' she said. 'It's just that I feel that I can relax with you.'

'I'm glad. I'd like to see more of you.'

'We can meet,' she said. 'Periodically.'

He smiled at 'periodically' as Ivan Shepherd had done.

'We can bitch about the Institute,' she said.

'General Newhouse thinks your project is super.'

'I'd like to stuff it to him,' Lauren said. 'I certainly never expected the head of the Institute to be a general. It feels like the army.'

Julian said, 'His war memoirs have been compared to *The Seven Pillars of Wisdom*.'

'I've got a theory that it's very unlucky for a woman to read that book.'

Julian smiled in a surrendering way, and she knew she had him.

'I think the General hates the research fellows. I wish they'd get rid of him.'

Julian said, 'Americans come to a new situation and say, "I don't like it. They'll have to change it." '

'What do English people say?'

' "I don't like it. Therefore, I'll have to change." '

Lauren said, 'I always think insecurity or a lack of confidence makes people susceptible to imitation. Weak people haven't got the guts to be themselves. But being yourself is being original! I like myself the way I am.'

She found her face in the coffee shop mirror.

She said, 'Still, he gives good parties.'

'You only get invited to one. It's a sort of welcome.'

'That's awful!' she said. 'That's another reason I hate him.'

She spent the afternoon trying to follow up the reference she had found in the Chinese newspaper, about the trade delegation from the Peoples Republic. She wondered whether Julian was telling the truth about the General – did he really think her project was super? 'Recycling Oil Revenue' was her working title. Arabs were so much more cooperative than the Chinese, and the Gulf was nearer and sunnier and didn't smell of mud and smoke, as China did. She reminded herself that she did not hate the Chinese; but they irritated her – the thought of them, so many of them – and she smirked, remembering Mr Van Arkady saying, 'There are two people in China.' She thought: Or one.

Alone, with no one watching her, she did not want to read. On the tube this morning with that young man across the aisle she had had no trouble concentrating on the *Renmin Ribao* – she'd had great concentration. Now she had none, and the English she was trying to read looked incomprehensible.

At five she saw General Newhouse leave. She put on her coat and followed him to the pavement, where a taxi was waiting.

'Is that your taxi, General?'

'Yes, can I give you a lift?'

They rode in silence towards Victoria. Lauren said, 'Your party was fun. I really liked your friends.'

The General stared at her, and then he said, 'We were glad you were able to come.'

She said, 'We must do it again sometime.'

He squinted at this, as if she had just lapsed into another language.

She said, 'By the way, my research is going wonderfully.' She wanted to mock his indifference by lying to him.

'I sometimes think that wealthy Arabs in London are the strangest phenomenon of our century. And someday they won't exist, and no one will understand how this happened in our time.'

Lauren said, 'Isn't there a reception for those Arab information people tonight?'

'I'm on my way there now,' the General said. His face was set in a look of boredom. 'It's by invitation, I'm afraid.'

Lauren smiled, hating the creases in his face and the set of his mouth. She said, 'Unfortunately I can't go – I've got a very important meeting.'

Again, the General seemed to be having trouble translating her words.

They passed a shop in Victoria Street that had a sign that flashed *Sex Show* and *Live Acts*.

The General pretended not to see.

'They're nothing,' Lauren said. 'I saw a sex show in Florida that would take five years off your life.' Then she rapped on the driver's window and said, 'I'm getting out here,' and she did, without another word, leaving the General to pay.

*

The plumber was late and unapologetic. He looked suspicious and a bit amateur. He had no tools with him. He made Lauren feel like a crank and then she was afraid and sorry she had let him in. But when he saw the toilet he sighed and she was encouraged: now he understood. The ice had thawed to the size of a grapefruit, but it had cracked a pipe.

He said, 'That'll need replacing.'

What was he pointing at?

'Do whatever needs to be done.'

'Who's the landlord here?'

'His name is Reggie. He's in Jamaica at the moment. But I can look after myself.'

The man said something in a low voice. When they were saying something very rude you could never understand them.

He went outside and returned with a bag of tools – a heavy one: it thudded and rattled the windows when he dropped it. He was clumsy – banging, thumping, throwing things down.

There was a kind of noise-making that was a clear sign of stupidity in a man.

Lauren sat by the electric fire in the other room, still wearing her coat. The clatter from the hall turned to silence. The last noise was the toilet flushing.

'It's working,' he said, stepping into the room.

'You're marvellous.'

He hesitated. 'Twenty-seven pounds,' he said. 'That in-cludes parts and labour.' He tore a sheet of paper from a pad – the bill. But she did not look at it.

She said, 'Your parts?'

She went to a cupboard and poured a measure of whisky. She gave it to him, she clinked glasses – hers was empty.

'Go on,' she said. 'I don't drink.'

'This won't do you any harm,' he said, and sipped, and his face tightened at the taste of it.

'You're a fast worker,' she said.

'I reckon I am,' he said, and sat down. He had begun to prowl.

'What's your name?'

'Pete.'

'Sneaky Pete,' she said. 'Like another drink?' She took a step towards his chair. 'I want to pay you.' And took another step. 'I mean, I want you to be satisfied.'

He smiled sheepishly, as if he had been discovered naked, and then he grunted, and sipped the drink again. He was waiting for her to do all the work.

Lauren touched the back of his hand, and then moved sinuously around his chair.

'What are you doing?'

[24]

'The dirty boogie. That's what we used to call it.' She knelt in front of him and said, 'I think I know what you want.' She unbuckled his belt. He did not object. 'I want to please you.'

He simply stared, and then he looked around and turned the lamp off. He did nothing more for a while. She fumbled with him, then held him tightly and used her tongue and her lips. She felt a sense of power, almost of magic – a kind of conjuring: she held this whole man in her mouth.

The man cried out, and then pushed himself back in the chair, as if slightly wounded – surprised by a burn.

Lauren stood up and switched on the lamp. She wiped a glistening fleck from her cheek, she straightened her dress; she had not removed her coat.

His trousers were down. He was limp, he looked weak and silly and unprotected. Lauren helped him to his feet and reminded him that his bag of tools was next to the chair. He looked at her in a shy amazed way, and then he laughed softly. He was pleased, and he had become grateful and boyish. All his rudeness was gone.

Lauren was holding the bill. She said, 'Now you'll mark that "paid", won't you?'

When he was gone she did her exercises and the room felt warmer. She had a bath. She ate alone: yogurt, an apple, some walnuts, a slice of toasted wholemeal bread and peanut butter, and a cup of herb tea.

Another day – and in many respects it had been typical. For over a month she had been living like this – on nothing – and hating it.

3

London was bad air and a sour mood, and on some days its clammy discomfort made her feel physically deformed; on other days she felt the city was poisoning her. But she was fighting it. She jogged down Acre Lane to Clapham and ran around the common listening to The Stranglers sing 'Shah Shah a Go Go' on her Sony Walkman; then she jogged home and had a long bath; and then breakfast of tea and melon, and bran mixed with yogurt. Each thing – the run, the bath, the food – made her purer and stronger. She was reassured, knowing she could keep her health in this senile city.

She wanted to move out of Brixton – this black district made her feel like a failure. She wondered whether she should leave the city altogether. It would mean leaving Britain – it was London or nothing; but the only habitable part of London, as far as she could see, was Mayfair. A man at the party had asked her why she liked it – was it that Giles something from the Foreign Office or had it been Van Arkady? Anyway, she'd said, 'It's really nice – it's just like Georgetown.'

The rest of Britain was dreary, especially Hull, where Lenny – he hated to be called Lenny – still sat, trying to explain China to his students. Once they had gone to Cornwall. The English talked about Cornwall the way Americans

[26]

spoke of California, but when she got to Padstow Lauren said, 'Are we here?' There was no sun. It was wet and windy, and the sharp ugly rocks made swimming dangerous. She laughed in a hard shouting way when someone mentioned that King Arthur and Sir Lancelot had lived there. 'And Confucius used to live in China!' she said.

Why were English rooms so cold? She had not been in a warm room once – a really warm room, where she could have taken off her clothes and padded around naked. When she grumbled or got sad about that she thought of 'The Cremation of Sam McGee'. She had recited it for the performing part of the Miss Virginia pageant, when she was Miss Culpeper. Miss Goochland played the clarinet but Miss Norfolk won with her roller skates. The Northern Lights had seen queer sights but the queerest they ever did see were those other finalists, and Lauren had looked at them and thought: You're all dogmeat.

She had begun to feel that same disgust in London and she now saw that it had been a mistake to skip yesterday's seminar. But she had had no way of knowing that a study tour to the Middle East was being set up. It would be a good way of leaving London and continuing her project. At the moment she felt shut out and ignored and very cold – the jerks were sitting on her head, and the nice ones were no use at all. She wanted to drop everything and go to the Middle East: she imagined white skyscrapers and clean sand and blinding light. She had no money, but she could find some. The idea was to make a decision and then act. The money would come. She had never felt so left out, and that morning she went to the Institute determined to put things in order.

Julian was already in the office, reading at his desk. There were post-graduate fellows who, when they were studying, looked exactly like timid priests – sort of praying over their books. That was the way Julian folded his hands when he read.

Lauren said, 'I'm going on the tour.'

Julian said he was surprised that she could be so confident of being selected. He pretended to be joking, but he was serious and sort of issuing a warning. He himself did not know whether he would be chosen. They were very fussy, he said.

'Then they're sure to want me,' Lauren said.

*

The organizer of the study tour, the man called Haseeb, was attached to the Kuwait Embassy. Lauren dialled the number that Julian had given her. She got a crossed line and a wrong number before it even rang, and then no one picked up the phone. She tried again nearer noon and got an engaged signal. Ten minutes later a secretary said that Mr Haseeb was out to lunch. Lauren thought: How can you get out without coming in? At three o'clock he had not returned; at four the number was engaged again; at four-thirty he was in a meeting. And then no answer: the office was closed, and Lauren realized that she had spent the entire day unsuccessfuly trying to make one lousy phone call.

The next day was Friday – no work for Muslims; but, being Arabs in London, they had Saturday and Sunday off, too. On Monday the secretary said that Mr Haseeb was out of the office. What was that supposed to mean? Bosses turned their secretaries into liars and guard dogs. People like Haseeb yawned over a magazine and said, 'Say I'm in a meeting.'

Because of these frustrations – not being able to see or speak to the man who could help her – Lauren imagined Haseeb very clearly. He was a brown balding man with a warty face and big teeth; in an English suit, and he weighed two hundred and eighty pounds. He had to wear a special sort of orthopaedic shoe because of his weight, and he had trouble getting out of most cars. He stank of cigarettes. He persecuted his huge wife.

On Tuesday the secretary told Lauren that Mr Haseeb was away for the day.

He had hairy knuckles. His eyes were two different colours. There was scurf on his collar.

'He's on holiday,' the secretary said on Wednesday.

Eating like a pig, and sneaking alcohol. His farts sounded like air brakes.

Then Lauren could not work. In the week since she had made up her mind to go on the Middle East study tour Lauren had put her work aside, because she had been waiting. She could not think or even read a simple article when she was in suspense – it really was like hanging in the air.

'We'll send you an application,' the secretary said on Thursday. Another Thursday and she was on the phone with the same question!

Lauren said, 'I understand they're choosing the candidates next week.'

'Mr Haseeb didn't leave me any instructions.'

'Would it speed things up if I came over and picked up the application in person?'

'Obviously.'

The secretary said this word in that tone of voice because she thought she could get away with it.

'You just missed him,' the secretary said when Lauren entered the foyer. Now she saw the secretary's name: *Miss Humpage*.

Lauren went to the window. The secretary was behind her, gloating – Lauren could feel the heat of it.

The young Arab getting into a black Jaguar wore a dark suit, and a tie like an orchid, and had the physique of a tennis player, and could not have been more than thirty. He looked back at the building and Lauren, who stepped nearer the window, put her hands on her hips and in this way opened her coat. But Haseeb had not seen her – couldn't possibly, or he would not have driven away.

The application called for an academic transcript, and – to satisfy the visa requirements of some of the countries on the tour's itinerary – it asked for a baptismal certificate, as well as a letter from the candidate's bank manager.

Lauren said, 'How am I supposed to get a baptismal certificate?'

'In the usual way, one would think,' Miss Humpage said, coldly. 'By being baptised.'

Did secretaries speak like this because of the awful people they worked for?

Lauren said, 'It's bureaucratic and bigoted.' Miss Humpage did not react. 'It's very demeaning.' Miss Humpage put a sheet of paper into the typewriter. 'And it'll take months.

[30]

Mine has to come from the States. And what's this about a letter from my bank?'

'Again, that is a visa requirement – we need proof that you have a balance of two hundred pounds in your account.'

'Is that supposed to be a lot of money?'

'I wouldn't know,' Miss Humpage said, lowering her tensed fingers to the keyboard.

'Then I'll tell you,' Lauren said. 'It's not.'

Lauren was grinning, but she did not have this money in her bank account.

'I want to make an appointment with Mr Haseeb.'

Miss Humpage said, 'Fill up this form. Just your name and a number where we can reach you. And your reason for the appointment.'

Lauren did as she was directed, writing fast.

Miss Humpage said, 'Is that a business or a home number?'

'It's the green phone,' Lauren said.

Miss Humpage did not react. She read aloud, ' "To investigate the pattern of petrodollar investment –" '

Lauren hated this, the woman reading at her from her own application.

' "– by OPEC agencies in development projects –" '

She spoke in a bored weary way, and at once the project seemed artificial and unnecessary. Miss Humpage looked up from the application.

' "– in Third World Muslim states." '

'And when Mr Haseeb is sober and decides to show up, tell him to take that application and shove it up his ass – unless you'd rather do that for him, too.'

*

On her way back to the Institute, and feeling frail, she entered a red telephone box that was full of stinks and tried to call Mr Van Arkady's bank. She spoke to his assistant. She heard the words 'in a meeting' and knew it was untrue. What were these people really doing who said they were in a meeting?

The man said, 'What is this in connection with?'

Lauren had called the number without knowing why, but the man's direct question made her realize that she wanted Mr Van Arkady's help and friendship. He was confident and worldly wise; he had contacts; he had money. He would sit down and tell her exactly what to do. Now she hated being alone. Six weeks in London she had not made one friend, but she did not regard this man Van Arkady as a stranger.

'It's a personal matter. We're friends.'

'I'll take your name and we'll get right back to you.'

She said, 'He doesn't know my name.'

'Didn't you say you were friends?'

'Oh, yes. We are.' Then she faltered. 'Only I didn't get a chance to tell him my name.'

After a silence, the man said, 'I see.'

'It's Mopsy Slaughter, but forget it.'

Then she hung up.

*

'I've got a feeling I'm not going on that study tour,' she said to Julian later, in the smoky, noisy pub. It was almost six o'clock. Julian was drinking a pint of beer. Lauren had a glass of Malvern water. 'I like to buy glasses of water,' she had said and the barman thought she was mocking him.

Julian had a long withered sausage on a chipped plate. He seemed to regard it as a problem. He kept glancing at it but he did not touch it.

He said, 'You don't need to go on the tour. You could probably find everything you need right here. Isn't that why you came to London?'

She said, 'London isn't London.'

'Ah, yes,' Julian said in the self-mocking way that came so easily to him, 'we are not what we were.'

'Don't feel bad. Tokyo isn't Tokyo, and Peking certainly isn't Peking, and Moscow isn't Moscow. Singapore isn't Singapore either. But, Jesus, Calcutta really is Calcutta.'

'I hope Berlin is Berlin,' he said.

'Half of it is.'

'I have to go there fairly soon to look into some archives on Arabia.'

She said, 'All you think about is work.'

'What do you think about?'

'Don't laugh, but I think about my body,' she said. 'The really important things like running, eating, sleeping and washing. I mean, doing them right. Who gives a shit about our research? I'd rather run a marathon.'

In his bewilderment at what she was saying Julian had overcome his nervousness with the sausage and had begun to eat it.

Lauren said, 'How can you put that thing into your mouth?'

'I suppose it *is* pretty disgusting,' he said.

She said, 'Why doesn't the stupid General invite us to another goddamned party? I really hate him.'

[33]

Julian watched her with the sausage sticking out of his mouth like a cigar, not biting down on it.

'Eat it and get it over with!' Lauren said. 'You're driving me crazy with that thing.'

When he was done and had wiped his hands she asked him for a loan of five pounds, which he gladly gave her.

*

The same evening of this long day Lauren was doing her stretching exercises on the floor and heard Lindsay from upstairs shouting that a bloke wanted her on the telephone – English bloke, Cockney-like. Lindsay always gave information in a meddling way. He was from Barbados and always barefoot indoors and had wet glistening eyes. He studied karate.

'It's me – Pete.' The voice was confident and casually familiar.

She said, 'I don't know anyone by that name.'

'The plumber.' Then he cleared his throat. 'Remember?' He cleared his throat again. 'I did that job at your place.'

She said, 'You're the person who fixed my toilet.'

'Yeah,' he said. 'Thought I might come over.'

'I don't need a plumber.'

'Thought you might like a drink.'

She said, 'I don't drink.'

She heard him gumming and ungumming his lips.

'Thought maybe we could get together.'

She said, 'Sorry,' and nothing more.

He became cross. 'Well, what about the last time?'

[34]

'That was strictly business.'

This silenced him. He tried again, but hungrily this time. 'I want to see you.'

She said, 'I don't know you. You performed a job for me and I paid you. I don't owe you anything.' And she hung up.

That phone call angered her, but she felt better after a bath, and then she sat in her mink-lined coat with the electric fire on, drying her hair. As the room warmed up old odours were stirred – food, sex, and dirt, all the human smells, the heat revealing the room's former tenants, the sour residue of their lives. London wasn't even pleasant when it was warm.

*

It was Thursday once more. That was the awful thing about failure: it humiliated you again and again by repeating the same empty days. She thought: I should have done Sino-Soviet relations – Chinese grants were easy these days – already people were sick of going to China. Then, remembering China, she saw Leonard's nose. Or the EEC, she thought: Paris was still Paris. She saw herself lecturing at a podium in Paris or Brussels, wearing her blue high-necked dress and white shoes. Then she thought: I would like to run a big hotel catering to the business traveller – he has special needs.

Julian entered the office from the library. He walked stiffly – he had been reading in his prayerful posture. Lauren knew that a mistake would be made and that he would be chosen by that little queer Haseeb to go on the study tour. She pitied Julian – he was wrong, incredibly naive, painfully truthful and timid, and always apologizing.

'Want a drink?' he said, in his embarrassed way, as if expecting her to say no.

She said, 'When you offer me a drink you actually mean something to drink.'

'Yes,' he said.

'But with other people, yes to a drink means yes to everything. And why is it always a drink?'

Julian had begun to look hopeful.

He was rummaging in his briefcase. 'This came for you this morning,' he said, and handed her a rectangular parcel in a padded bag. 'I signed for it. It came by messenger.'

'Just a book.'

'Okay then?' he said. 'The Duke of York?'

She said no in a resigned way and went home in the dark, leaving all her library books and her file of photocopies on her desk.

*

It was not a book. It was a book-shaped video recording. It had no label, and the parcel had no return address. She had a small black and white television set, but no video machine. Lindsay had one. He was a member of a Brixton video club; he rented pornographic videos, and ones about karate, and Nazi prison camps. His favourite was one called *I Spit on Your Grave*: rape and murder.

'Hello, stranger,' Lindsay said. He was dressed like the kung-fu hero on the poster near his bed.

She said, 'I want to borrow your video machine. All that

means is I want to borrow your video machine. Don't offer me a so-called drink.'

'You're a really funny kid. I rate you.'

Lindsay stood up. What was there about karate that attracted undersized people? Lauren took a step back.

'Just the machine,' she said.

4

She watched the videotape in her room as she did her stretching exercises – naked, on a long straw mat, the blinds down, and the electric fire blazing and filling the room with dusty heat. Her exercises were like a dancer's warm-up – flexing her arms, and tugging one heel and then the other against her stomach, and finally salaaming slowly towards the television screen.

– *This young woman earns two hundred pounds an hour.*

The narrator spoke in a flat insulted voice and the film showed a woman hurrying through strolling groups of people in Park Lane. It was not a cheaply made film. It was a television documentary, well-edited and with good sound – perhaps a BBC programme that had been taped. The woman was seen from a number of angles, and Lauren noticed that she was very ordinary and overdressed, with podgy shoulders and a chubby chin and a big bum. Dogmeat.

– *Her takings for a single week might be several thousand pounds* –

'And she weighs three hundred pounds,' Lauren said, stretching.

Now the woman was introducing herself to a swarthy moustached man who actually looked impressed and grateful – his libido on the boil and his tail wagging. The poor man was half the woman's size and he stood in his tiny Italian suit on stiff skinny legs.

– She is one of a growing number of young women who work in London's newest industry – the escort service –

His tone was interesting. It attempted stifled horror and distaste, but Lauren didn't believe it – she was sure the narrator was as fascinated as she was. With hidden cameras and bugged phones, the film progressed in a patchwork way, explaining the various girls-for-hire agencies that operated in Central London.

The girls looked unattractive and stupid – and they were certainly overpaid. Large sums were mentioned, but Lauren was still new enough to England to think of plain shapeless lumps whenever she heard the word pounds.

– It's much more than they're worth, said a cherubic hooker in dark glasses. *That's why it's not prostitution!*

– I agree. This was a soft-voiced black woman with a vast shiny handbag. *Prostitution is lowering yourself like, but this is just the opposite.*

The customers seemed to Lauren unexpectedly young and well-off. The ones who were interviewed were excited at the prospect of meeting a girl. Most of the men were foreign, many were from the Middle East, a few were Americans. And an Englishman – but then Lauren remembered that this was England.

– I like the simplicity of it, one of the American men said. *I hate hassles.*

The man looked like Archie McComb from Culpeper – just as big and pleasant, the same beer belly, the same spiky hair. But this one had money.

– Usually it's just a bite of something, the man explained. *You get lonely. It's company. Sure, a bite of something and then you take a hike.*

[39]

It was apparently a discreet business – practically all the arrangements were made by telephone. The makers of the film stage-managed an appointment. The narrator's tone of voice prepared the viewer in a sarcastic way for a kind of viciousness; but Lauren found the operation reassuring and practical, if a little comic.

– *Jasmine Agency. May I help you?* The voice at the end of the line seemed trapped in a small bottle.

– *I'm ringing from the Hilton,* the man in the foreground said. Hyde Park was visible out the window. *I'd like an escort for the evening. For dinner and, um –*

– *Give us your name and room number and we'll ring you right back.*

– *Why is that necessary?*

–*It's just a precaution, sir.*

Of course, Lauren thought. The man gave the information and then put the phone down. When it rang again he resumed.

– *I'd like to know how much it costs.*

– *One hundred pounds, plus twenty-five agency fee.*

– *What happens then?*

– *The rest is by arrangement with the lady. Shall I book an escort for you?*

The screen went black, the sound became echoey, and now it was as if the cameraman was squashed behind a door and squinting out. A doorbell rang loudly; there was gabbling, and the indistinct motion of several humans, and the friendly scrape of a Scottish voice.

– *We don't take personal cheques.*

When this woman crossed in front of the camera Lauren

could see that she was expensively dressed, with an unnecessary and rather flashy scarf. But physically she was very plain.
She had freckles and fat knees and she was definitely uneducated.

– *Mind if I smoke?* she said, lighting one.

Lauren laughed at the stupidity of it – the silly woman
stinking up the small hotel room with her cigarette, and then
coughing into her stubby fingers as she counted the man's
money.

– *What did you say your name was?*

– *Samantha. Samantha Buckingham.*

Lauren jeered at her. 'Samantha Buckingham! I love it!'

– *Pleased to meet you. I'm Frank Harris. I want to take you to a
party.*

– *I like a good party,* the woman said, and Lauren smiled at
the accent – how ignorant and ridiculous it was.

– *Then maybe later we can pop back here for a nightcap. You
don't mind that, do you?*

– *Might cost you extra, depending on the time. Do you always
talk this much? There's nothing to be nervy about, darling.*

The next shot was of a party in the ballroom of a London
hotel, a throng of shouting people – women in bright gowns
and men in dark suits.

– *Most of the women in this room are social escorts being paid
anywhere from fifty to five hundred pounds to stand and smile. In
some cases, rather more is required.*

Their faces were crusted with make-up; they had gooey
lips and lacquered piles of hair. Lauren saw mingled greed
and gratitude in their eyes. And she thought they were
pathetic – not for their lack of style or their silly sequined

dresses, but for their heavy flesh and dull skin. They were hideously unhealthy.

The camera moved to a bright-eyed Arab at the party trying to speak to one of the girls and mumbling shyly.

– *Here, what do you call that, then?* the girl said, jerking the lower edge of his headdress.

'A ghotra,' Lauren said.

– *Ghotra,* the man said. *It is for the sun and sand and windstorm.*

– *Very useful in London that!* The girl screamed with laughter.

Slob, Lauren thought; but the man was gently laughing with the girl.

– *The Jasmine Agency has been operating for three years from their offices in Shepherd Market. Every evening of the year girls are dispatched to customers in London's hotels.*

The narrator described the innocent-seeming premises of the Jasmine Agency, and their mysterious directors, as a small figure hurried out of the office door and approached a Daimler that had just drawn up to the kerb.

– *This is Captain Twilley. He has been a farmer in Rhodesia and a sultan's bodyguard in the Persian Gulf. He has twice been arrested for firearms offenses – carrying an unlicensed revolver and being in possession of a stolen weapon. There is no record of his having earned the title 'captain'.*

A young and rather haggard woman emerged from the Daimler. Captain Twilley took her by the arm and escorted her to the door.

– *Madame Cybele. Her last known employer was The Hotel Bristol, Beirut, Lebanon, though her duties were somewhat obscure.*

A reporter suddenly appeared in the foreground of this shot, startling the woman.

— *I have a few questions for you.*

The woman recovered and gave him a corrosive stare.

— *I cannot help you.*

Her voice was faintly foreign, and her slight accent and the over-correct English made her seem all the more rude.

Captain Twilley loomed.

— *On your bike!* he shouted at the reporter.

The Captain had bushy eyebrows and a tweed tie and wore a thick baggy suit which had a bristly nap and a weave like sacking.

— *Certain aspects of your business seem rather strange to us.*

— *Stranger things happen at sea,* Captain Twilley said.

Madame Cybele's pale weary face was framed by a black fur collar. She had large eyes and large lips, and Lauren was interested to see that someone so young and attractive could also look so used up.

— *You will excuse us, please?* Madame Cybele said.

Captain Twilley shielded her and swept her into the offices of the Jasmine Agency.

This was not the end of the videotape. There were sequences of women at dances and dinner parties, and shopping in the West End — smiling at tiny watches on trays; they were shown at embassy functions, in restaurants, and at national day receptions under multi-coloured flags and banners. They were all paid for this.

Lauren was struck by how plain they were, how little conversation they had; their accents were uneducated and their health was mediocre; they had bad skin and wore too

[43]

much make-up. They had heavy legs. They smoked. They were dogmeat.

She had stopped doing her exercises. She sat cross-legged, naked on the mat, still watching. And for the duration of the film London seemed a habitable city – it was human and workable. What had been incomprehensible to her before was now clear. She saw order: a pattern was revealed – motives and results, too, and for the first time something potentially friendly. The city no longer seemed foreign and half dead to her. She was thinking how much prettier and better she was than those women, and how powerful she could be. When the tape ended she felt invigorated with a peculiar strength. In this foreign place she saw something familiar and alive. And the most important thing of all: in this huge city of strangers someone knew her very well. It was the person who had sent the tape, and Lauren felt that this person – he or she – was still whispering encouragement to her.

*

Lauren tried on her Thai-silk dress, pale yellow with bright stripes, and her Italian shoes – two narrow straps and a three-inch heel that was so sharp it jammed in escalators. Her shoulders were bare, her hair upswept, and her thickest gold chain round her neck – Noosie, the Brixton neck-freak, had drawn it tight and photographed the welt it had left. Now Lauren posed in front of her full-length mirror and smiled: Party time! She had worn this dress to a cocktail party at the Hemisphere Institute and to General Newhouse's dinner party. She knew that as a political economist she was disconcerting in it, and she loved the tactical advantage in being disconcerting.

This dress would not do – it wasn't right. When she took it off, the rustle of silk and the sight of her own nakedness aroused her. She felt queenly. Then she parted her legs and teased herself with one fingertip and she shuddered with pleasure at the white length of her body.

She put on a dark tartan kilt, and a white pleated shirt that she buttoned to her neck. She drew on her oatmeal tweed jacket.

She said, 'I think this recession can be explained by a credulous over-dependency on supply-side theory.'

She fastened her grandmother's brooch onto her lapel and turned back to the mirror.

'On the other hand, in China until very recently all external debts were settled immediately in cash, taking no notice at all of the float possibilities.'

She tugged her hair back and wound it and fixed it with an old tortoiseshell clasp – her 'librarian clasp'; and she glanced again at the mirror.

'Petrodollars are definitely bottoming out. If they hit the tape at one-twenty your oil producers may begin to sell gold.'

She pulled on her boots and stood up and stamped in them.

'As seen from Mayfair, the downside risk is lethal but worth taking.'

And lastly she put on a pair of gold-rimmed glasses.

'I'm now a virgin,' she said. 'You break it – you pay for it.'

It was ten o'clock in the morning. At one, a Fellows' meeting was scheduled in the Situation Room of the Institute

– cheap wine and cheese sandwiches and a pep talk from the General. There was time, there was time.

The videotape had suggested sumptuous offices by showing a plaster façade painted in the dead white of a Nash terrace and with ornate grillework, and the sort of pompous brass name-plate that the Institute itself had mounted over its porcelain bell-push. This one said *Jasmine Agency*.

Lauren rang and entered – as a smaller notice demanded – but instead of stepping into comfortable space and warm light she found herself at the bottom of a steep flight of stairs. And it was chilly, too – like being at the bottom of a well.

On the landing high above her were two men in robes, snatching at their heads in frustration. It was an Arab gesture that looked like a frenzied benediction. They were speaking to a receptionist, who was seated at a small desk with her morning paper and her cup of tea. Lauren had expected to see Madame Cybele at the top of the stairs and she was disappointed by the girl at the desk – another bulgy bitch, like the ones in the programme.

Each of the men – she now clearly saw that they were Arabs – wore an English suit jacket over his white robe. They were jabbering in a hurt, puzzled way. The language barrier so often made foreigners look stubborn or childish – it was what Lauren hated most about having to speak other languages: she felt infantile saying 'Please' and 'Thank you' and 'Very good' and all that talk in the present tense, like a silly novel trying to look brisk and important.

Lauren shut the front door and the men stopped talking as the door-slam reached them. Now they looked down the steep stairwell at Lauren rising.

[46]

'Hi!' she said. She was smiling and even after that long climb she was not winded.

The men backed away as if to receive her, and one blinked in satisfaction and said, 'We want this one.'

*

It was the first time she had ever been early for a Fellows' Meeting. She sat primly, waiting for the others. They entered self-consciously, heaving briefcases and not speaking – Julian, Fairman from the Asia Section, Stringer, Willymot, and Brigid Doyle, an affected girl ('ashoom' she said instead of 'assume') with broken teeth who rode an old bike and never took off her greasy raincoat. Apart from Julian, they all hated Lauren: Fairman because she had been to Chengdu, Willymot because she had stuck him with a restaurant bill their first week, Stringer because she had borrowed his cheap fountain pen and lost it; and Doyle – obvious.

Julian whispered, 'Any luck with your application?'

'What application?'

'Haseeb,' he said. 'That Kuwaiti chap. The Study Tour.'

This delighted her. She had completely forgotten all that. She said, 'Fuck it!'

Julian pinched his face. He did not understand.

She said, 'Don't care!'

The General entered and addressed them in a tone that was both bullying and patronizing, speaking of their research projects (fat Brigid was doing famine relief!). What Lauren hated most about his tone was that it showed no trust in them, no interest, only a sort of vague irritation that these research

Fellows existed; and, all the while he spoke, he wore the expression of a man who hears a mosquito buzzing but can't see the creature he is impatient to swat.

'Finally,' he said in the little homily he always saved for last, 'the Arab world. A word. I don't have to tell you that it's on our own doorstep. I know some of you' – he looked at Lauren – 'have met with a certain resistance. Don't be discouraged and above all don't be foolishly suspicious or wrong-headed. Your efforts will be considerable but so will your rewards. The Institute's relationship with the Arab world has grown out of an unprejudiced enthusiasm for the land and its peoples, and should any of you decide to pursue your researches further it would give the Institute a tremendous strategic advantage in applying for gifts from Arab agencies trading in the UK –'

The two men had taken her to the coffee shop of the Hilton and bought her a cup of espresso and a large piece of Black Forest gâteau. They took her protests for friendly excitement, and she said no so vigorously they ordered her a second piece of cake. She broke the first cake apart in a ceremonial way, to show she was grateful; but she did not taste it, nor did she drink the coffee. When she ate even a tiny morsel of something she didn't like she could taste it for two days.

Each of the men ate a slice of baklava, and then one wiped his mouth on his handkerchief and said, 'We go?' to Lauren.

They left the other man at the table grinning at his wristwatch. He had shown Lauren the watch. Its face was a solid gold ingot weighing fifteen grams. He had also, that same morning, bought a large stuffed bear and an air pistol. The teddy bear was for his wife, he said tenderly, and he was going to shoot birds with the air pistol. There were many birds in his country – many, many birds to shoot at. He was still yapping about bird shooting when his heavier friend swallowed and said, 'We go?'

'What's in the bag?' she asked.

He whisked it open as if at a customs' check.

'A book!' she said. 'What's the title?'

An Arab with a book: it half scared her.

'No, no,' he was saying, and pulled it out. He lifted one of the hard covers and plinking music began, the first few bars of 'The Floral Dance' but even a few bars was enough to get this man wagging his head happily.

'Ah, that's better – a music box,' Lauren said. 'A book is a pain in the ass, isn't it?'

The man was still wagging his head to *pinka-pink, pinka-pink*.

She could never tell the ages of foreigners. This man might have been thirty or forty, or more – she believed that middle-age was a certain musty soapy odour, and he had it on him. He gave her a hundred pounds in twenties from a canvas money belt that looked as if it held slugs of ammo. Then he went to the bathroom and washed noisily, and he stood by while Lauren washed, supervising her in a fussy way that had nothing to do with sex. When she lay naked on the bed, he knelt between her legs and lifted his robe. He had not taken it off even to wash. His penis was thick and dark and looked like an old pickle. He entered her, pushing hard, and only minutes later he ground his teeth, and cried, 'Allah!' and was done.

She was washing, using the bidet, when the second man

slipped into the room. She had left the bathroom door open in order to keep an eye on her handbag, and then she saw this second man come towards her to watch. And the hotel room door slammed: that was the first man leaving. They had it all worked out!

Without speaking, this man took a sock-like purse from his pocket and a plug of bills from the purse. When she had finished washing herself, he handed it over. Lauren took five long strides to the bed and tumbled in. The man peeled off his skullcap and massaged his shaven head as he contemplated her. Something was wrong – he seemed distracted, at once modest and impatient. She reached for him but he drew back, keeping his hands from her, as if fearing contamination. Then he shuffled towards her and gave her a little slap on her hip – an animal pat. It was an order. She understood and turned on her stomach.

'Take it easy,' she said, facing the headboard and seeing his dim reflection in the varnished wood.

But he had started with his finger and already it hurt. He was lost in a gabbling monologue with himself, and using her hip bones as handles he shoved himself into her abruptly, surprising her.

The swiftness and the slight pain made Lauren sob, which seemed to please the man. He pushed in deeply and rode her and then lay the length of her with his teeth clamped on her neck and squealing softly like a sudden rabbit.

'Any questions,' she heard the General saying.

She frowned, remembering, then said, 'No, sir.'

*

[50]

She had agreed to meet Captain Twilley at the Jasmine Agency that evening. The videotape was still so fresh in her mind that she felt as if she was part of the same film – but a vast improvement over those tacky English girls and that fat Scot who had coughed as she had counted her money.

Captain Twilley was much smaller in the flesh and very gruff.

He said, 'Escorts don't normally come to the agency, so don't make a habit of it. Use the telephone instead. We'll keep track of your appointments and send you a weekly invoice. That's all I need from you – your name and your telephone number. Your real name. We guarantee absolute discretion. If you want to use another name for work, that's fine. We don't ask awkward questions. This is like the Foreign Legion.'

'I want to use my real name.'

'That's very unusual.'

She said, 'I'm not ashamed of what I'm doing.'

Until that moment he had been scribbling on a pad and only glancing at her. But now he looked up and kept his eyes on her as he leaned back in his chair.

'You're a bright spark,' he said. 'But I'm less than ecstatic about your outfit.' He spun one finger in a winding motion that he intended as criticism. 'Have you got anything a little more colourful that would emphasize your figure?'

'If you think a social escort is just tits and a tight dress you have a very old-fashioned idea of what this job requires,' Lauren said.

'What have you got that it requires?' he asked.

She said, 'I'm user-friendly.'

[51]

'Good,' Captain Twilley said. 'We get all kinds of punters.'

The next night she was summoned to the Savoy by a tall French boy, eighteen at most, who greeted her in his room wearing a red baseball hat with limp cloth horns – like cow horns – sewn to its crown. Their meal was sent up. He ate in his underwear, the hat on his head. She peeled an orange and ate three segments. They watched television. He kept his money in a paper bag. 'Tarzans,' he said, stirring the ten pound notes. 'Tarzans.' He paid her and then went to sleep with his head in her lap. He woke and wept when she said she had to go home, and then he screamed and frightened her, and slammed the door as she walked quickly down the corridor.

She felt wonderful afterwards, as if she had walked a tightrope and won the grand prize. Her only regret was that she had to go all the way to Brixton to be home. She wanted something nearer – a flat in Mayfair – perhaps a short distance from the Institute; she wanted two lives separated by a few streets.

That same week she was sent an invitation to a reception at The Dorchester. It was to welcome a delegation from the Bahrain Ministry of Information. The minister himself was there, and so was the ambassador. The invitation had been delivered by a messenger to the Institute, and it was only when Lauren saw Captain Twilley waiting in the lobby that she was sure that she was representing the Jasmine Agency and not the Hemisphere Institute.

Captain Twilley took her upstairs and into the ballroom by a side door, bypassing the receiving line and a beefy-faced

Englishman with side-whiskers and a red frock coat who was shouting the names of the arriving guests.

'Look for Puddles,' Captain Twilley said, and hurried downstairs for another of his girls.

Lauren saw Madame Cybele approaching.

'Puddles?'

The woman's frown meant yes. But Lauren thought: if someone's called Puddles you don't ask why. Lauren liked Madame Cybele's dark eyes and cruel fleshy mouth, but something else disturbed her. The high collar of her dress did not quite hide a grey bruise on her neck – the top of the splotch just showed. This bruise, there, seemed to Lauren very decadent – what was it about necks that made men crazy?

'Follow me,' Madame Cybele said, and she snaked through the room. It was mostly men, and nearly all of them Arabs – in *besht* and *thobe* and red-flecked *ghotra*, like a desert gathering; and others in suits, and in various military uniforms. They were unusual clothes and made the party seem festive, like a fancy dress ball: these men dressed as Arab sheiks and those as potentates and those as stage-generals. Most of the men looked wealthy, and they had bad posture, as if they did nothing but sit or ride or be carried.

Madame Cybele stopped at a group of three men. Now she raised her voice and became charming. 'Gentlemen, I'd like you to meet a young friend of mine.'

Each man smiled and spoke his name quickly, like a sentence in Arabic.

'They're very generous, but ever so naughty,' Madame Cybele said, in an affected way that did not go with her intelligent eyes or her bruise. 'Be very careful, Lauren, they're from Kuwait.'

'I wonder whether you can tell me,' Lauren said to the men, 'what effect an Iran-Iraq war has had on the tribal people living in those immense marshes north of Basra and the Shatt-al-Arab waterway. I mean, the Madan and the Faraigat.'

The men stared at her, and then one spoke.

'Very trouble,' he said and put on a sorrowful expression.

Another said, 'Yes, too much trouble for them. But I am living in Bahrain today.'

'He keeps inviting me there,' Madame Cybele said. 'One of these days I'm going to surprise you and say yes.'

But Lauren was still closely attentive. She said to this man, 'I have great admiration for your pipeline.'

'Well, well,' Madame Cybele said.

'Awali to Dharan,' Lauren said.

'You'll excuse me,' Madame Cybele said, a trifle coldly, and slipped away.

'And Sitrah. And Jebel ad Dukhan,' the man said. 'You know Zahran.' He showed Lauren his foot. 'I buy this shoes in Zahran. This is the most expensive shoes in the world.'

'I hope you've got two of them,' Lauren said. 'Then you can show me around the Gulf and not get sore feet.'

'Please visit Kuwait,' the third man said. He had been watching with bright squirrel-like eyes, and smiling each time Lauren spoke. He was intelligent looking and had a good accent – none of this 'Very trouble' or 'zis shiss'. He was chafing a small string of worry beads in his fingers.

'Nice beads,' she said.

'Take them.' And he pressed them into her hand.

They were heavy and cool – perhaps jade, perhaps something even more precious. The clasp was gold. She smiled, feeling powerful again, because without any effort she was a success; and what could they possibly deny her when she was trying hard to please them – she knew that she had an unusual capacity to please men. It had everything to do with forgetting her own pleasure and being a willing slave.

'I wanted to go to Kuwait,' she said, handling the beads in her long fingers. 'But Haseeb at your embassy flatly refused to see me.'

'I have no embassy,' the man said.

'But you know Haseeb!' one of the other men said. 'Haseeb is just a small boy. And a lazy boy. I will arrange your visit. No Murphy's Law, no very trouble.'

'What do you think?' Lauren said to the man who had given her his worry beads.

'I think you should come with me,' he said, 'so that we can discuss this' – and he smiled – 'at the highest possible level.'

He pinched the tip of her elbow and steered her towards the door. Then he released her and hurried forward to embrace someone – another man. They kissed and greeted each other with great formality – murmuring; but whether it was English or Arabic she could not tell.

'Meet my friend.'

Who was being introduced – she or the man? Then it didn't matter. The man was Hugo Van Arkady.

At the General's he had seemed swarthy and heavy; in this gathering he looked thinner and rather pale and intense. But it was merely the difference in the setting, she was sure. He registered no surprise at seeing her.

'We've met,' Van Arkady said. 'And I was sure that we would meet again. You're keeping good company, Dr Slaughter. Don't let this man's enthusiasm discourage you.'

She said, 'You remembered my name!' She was pleased, for why would he bother to remember her name if he did not think she was one of his special number? It was magic more than memory: she was suddenly part of the city, and now everything in London seemed possible. That was an important moment for her – his easy assumption of friendship and her delight. And he didn't judge her, nor did he seem to care whether she was an escort or a research fellow. It was as if he had known her for a long time – that, rather than the other way around, because she also found him a little scary looking, and if she had not felt like a success she suspected that she might be afraid of him, as she had been – slightly – at the General's.

'We must make arrangements,' the man said.

Van Arkady said, 'You both look very happy. It is wonderful to see you – wonderful.'

In the nightclub the man said his name was Karim and that he hoped they would meet again soon. He said, 'I know what you want.'

She said, 'I want you.'

'That is a great deal,' he said. 'But if it makes you happy' – and he made a face at her at the dark and candlelit table.

'That man Van Arkady is an old friend of mine,' she said.

'Oh, yes,' he said. 'I could see.'

'But there's nothing to be jealous of,' she said.

Karim nodded gravely at this and then ordered a feast of lamb and chicken kebabs, with a great bowl of rice, and lemon soup.

Lauren did not eat anything. Karim picked at one kebab, but when he murmured that Lauren really ought to eat something – it was good, a traditional feast, it made you strong and lovely – when he said this, Lauren grasped a skewer.

'There's something sexy about these,' she said. 'The way it's raw where the skewer pierces the meat. I love these skewers. I even like the word skewers.'

These skewers were swords. Karim presented her with one, wiping it on his napkin and telling her to take it home.

'But why?' she said.

'Because you are my chicken.'

5

In the daytime there was the Institute, and at night the Agency, but she found the work similar in many respects; and when people (day or night) asked her what she did the rest of the time she said, 'Research,' and she thought: I've gone the whole nine yards.

She saw Karim often. It was always business. He said she should get a flat in London – he innocently believed that Brixton was not in London.

'I'd love a place in Mayfair. Halfway –'

She was going to say 'Halfway between the Institute and Park Lane', but she forced herself to be silent. She wanted to keep her two lives separate – she was superstitious in a routine way, and she was also practical. And she had succeeded in dividing her life: at the Institute she let everyone know that her real name was Mopsy, and they called her Mopsy; at the Jasmine Agency, and to most of the men she was sent to, she was Dr Slaughter – it was Van Arkady's greeting that had given her the idea. 'Cheerio, Mopsy!' Julian said at the Duke of York, and an hour later she would be speaking into a house phone at a hotel: 'This is Dr Slaughter. I'm in the lobby –'

'Halfway,' Karim was saying, urging her to finish her sentence.

'Halfway through Mayfair.'

[58]

'Yes, yes, yes.'

He was glad in the way that wealthy men became glad: she had never seen this in anyone else. These men had everything they wanted – they had so much that they could not imagine what someone else might want. They could grant any wish, and yet they lived in a rather saturated world in which people seldom expressed a wish. It was maddening for them, and that was why Lauren's saying 'I'd love a place in Mayfair' made Karim grateful.

A few days later he took her to a small flat in Half Moon Street, at the Piccadilly end, number three. Here he photographed her as she sat naked in clear plastic chairs or as she pedalled a Finnish exercise cycle. He took his pleasure that way, talking to her the whole time.

'Is this yours?'

The question embarrassed him: he was still taking pictures.

'The flat,' she said.

'You like it, don't you?'

She said, 'You know what I want.'

'Yes, Doctor.'

'You're an awful pimp,' she said.

She was just teasing, but he didn't laugh.

She thought a moment, still pedalling as Karim knelt with his camera, and she said, 'There are a lot of things I don't have. But I'm not greedy. I don't want a car. I'd rather have my own room and the freedom to do anything I want in it. I don't want to be bossed around. If there's one question I hate it's "Where have you been, young lady?" I don't care much about jewellery. I don't care about the things I'm being denied now. I want the things I was denied when I was twelve years old.'

There was as yet not much furniture in the flat on Half Moon Street, but even so she became attached to it, and she disliked having to leave it and take the tube to Brixton. These days Karim always used the flat, photographing her and talking. Was this sex? If so, it was the oddest slowest kind. Sometimes he took an hour or two. That was the trouble with the kinky ones – they needed time. The others were different. She prided herself on being able to blow an average guy and be at the door in fifteen minutes, shaking hands – that was always how they wanted it – and leaving. She was never kissed. Karim did not even touch her.

He shared her with his friends; they were bad and boring, but no worse than husbands – and they paid. She agreed to it because there was no jealousy, because it was business, and because with Karim's friends she was allowed to use the flat on Half Moon Street.

Often with these men there was no sex, but instead long noisy nights – too much food, and too much talk; and back in Brixton she fasted and exercised. The men were a useless combination of wealth and laziness, but they were so kind. They were always exposed, always waiting, always self-conscious and they always gave her too much money. She always felt she had the advantage. She still called it dating.

Some others were American – businessmen: they would answer the phone while she licked at them. 'I'm a little tied up at the moment – I'll get right back to you.' So many of them were vain about their hair, and one put on a rubber bathing cap before he got into bed with her. Another one told her in explicit detail how she was to take him into her mouth, and then he added sharply, 'But don't touch my hair.' They wore gold chains and expensive pendants around their necks. When they were violent or very stupid Lauren said, 'I've got to get up real early tomorrow!' and left quickly. If they protested at this, she said angrily, 'Don't you treat me like a hooker!' London was full of vulgar brainless bitches who would do anything for a weekend in Spain or a new pair of boots, but how many of these bitches had a masters in economics and a doctorate in international relations?

'I've just flown in from Hong Kong.'

'I've been there,' she said.

'I closed a pretty big deal.' They were both cautious and boastful.

She said, 'When I was in Hong Kong I was using the archives at the university. They've got some fantastic stuff on the Peoples Republic.'

But the men could be pathetic.

'My name's Lauren – what's yours?'

'Anthony J. Pistorino,' one man said.

He swallowed and blinked, because it was a lie – an hour later he forgot the name; but whenever she remembered it she laughed.

Another thing about the men was that they were seldom young. And when it was late and they were tired they looked older; their fatigue gave them a grief-stricken expression. Lord Bulbeck was like that – sorrowful eyes at midnight. He was well-known for his charity work and in his flat he kept photographs of himself receiving awards for his efforts. One night as Lauren was leaving Lord Bulbeck's flat in Queen's

Gate, she paused and peered at a photograph. The foot of some aeroplane steps: Lord B. hugging a white-haired man.

'He was a very important man.'

She said, 'Really?'

'A very great statesman,' he said, as if to a tame little whore.

Lauren said, 'Ben Gurion, yes. That whole issue makes me feel very leftwing. But, before you say he was greatly mis- understood, I will tiptoe away.'

Lord Bulbeck looked up, amazed that she knew the face.

She decided that he was a lonely man. He said he had no friends now and often did not feel safe. That was why he had gone to the Jasmine Agency, and that was also why – after the first few times – he would not accept anyone but Lauren. One evening he took her to dinner at Claridge's. He was celebrat- ing, he said. 'I'm seventy years old today.'

She said, 'I'm flattered that you included me.'

'There is no one else.'

Then she wanted to justify herself and gave him a little encouragement, too. She said, 'I've got a PhD, you know. In international relations. You didn't invite a dummy to your birthday party.'

He said, 'I know all about you. A man with my views has to take great precautions.'

'What sort of views?'

'The sort that are not changed by discussion,' he said, and that was that.

When he paid the bill he said, 'As a boy I used to walk past and see that man out front dressed in his fine uniform – his top hat and gold braid. I wanted so badly for him to tip his hat to me, and open the door. "Good evening, my lord." '

'But that's exactly what he did to you tonight.'

'Yes,' Lord Bulbeck said.

She said, 'I know just what you mean.'

He shook his head. He smiled at her, because it was too much trouble for him to explain. He began, saying, 'My father sold scrap iron in Limehouse. I was always a Labour man,' and then he gave up, though she knew that he was only trying to tell her that he had been made a Life Peer in one of the Honours Lists – did he really think an American wouldn't understand a simple thing like that?

She went home with him. She said, 'One of these days I'm going to take you to my place on Half Moon Street.'

'In the meantime, let us make do with a tango at Queen's Gate.'

Was it 'tango' or 'tangle'? Anyway, that was what he called it. She liked the way he talked. He said, 'Another bottoo of wine?' He said, 'Peepoo can be horriboo.'

These old men still had life left in them! They were slow to get started but could go on for ages. Lord Bulbeck always said, 'I've been planning this for days.' But another old man paid her double the rate to give her enemas.

He too had come through the agency. It made her wonder about security. But then she discovered an answer of sorts. She asked another girl at the party. 'Arabella' – they all had assumed names like that – just laughed.

'Security? Don't be silly – whatever for?'

They were so stupid! Lauren wanted to say, 'Don't you know that you're an incredible security risk?'

But they didn't know – so they weren't. Their stupidity was a form of security. And only Lauren knew that she needed a baptismal certificate and a bank statement and her grand-mother's maiden name on an application to go to some of these countries – but she could take all her clothes off and sit on the ambassador's face on the recommendation of Captain Twilley or 'Puddles'.

She knew that Captain Twilley found her cold.

He said, 'Karim likes you' or 'Lord Bulbeck wants you back' in a disbelieving way, and sometimes – not obscenely but with genuine curiosity – 'What have you *got*?'

'An education,' Lauren said. She did not like the man. He talked too much about the army.

He said, 'It doesn't take an education to get fucked.'

'No one fucks me,' she said, staring back at him. 'I do all the fucking. It used to annoy me, but now it suits me fine.'

She guessed that Captain Twilley must have told this to Madame Cybele – Lauren still could not bear to say the word 'Puddles'. The young pale woman invited her out for a drink and mentioned it: Lauren liked her big soft lips and idly imagined kissing and biting them. This was at The Ritz, both women drinking Perrier (four pounds for two glasses of water, but it was a lovely place) and Madame Cybele repeated Lauren's remark. It had been polished by the retelling and had the sound of a 'saying'.

Lauren said, 'I was thinking of Karim and his cameras. And that flat of his on Half Moon Street. Have you ever seen it?'

'He doesn't live in Half Moon Street,' Madame Cybele said.

'His studio, let's say,' Lauren said. 'I'd give anything to live there.'

'Don't ever say, "I'd give anything." It can be dangerous.'
Madame Cybele looked at her from across the table. 'I know.
I got here the hard way.'

Lauren said, 'That sounds awful.'

Madame Cybele seemed to read the questions in Lauren's
eyes. She said disgustedly, 'The things they say to you!'

Lauren said, 'I hate the ones who don't wash.'

Madame Cybele shrugged. Why was it that her bruises
never quite vanished, but lingered as faded inky stains on her
very white skin?

Lauren liked her for saying then, 'They never think about a
woman's pleasure.'

'All they ever want to do is bum me,' Lauren said. 'I always
come home feeling like I've been riding a bike – they're killing
my ass.'

Madame Cybele smiled – it was the first time Lauren had
ever seen her do so, and Lauren was encouraged to ask her
the question that had remained unanswered for weeks.

'Did you ever send me a videotape?'

'No.' But Madame Cybele became watchful.

'That's why I looked you up that first day. It was a
programme about escort agencies. Yours was in it.'

'I know. It was a stupid programme.'

'So who could have sent it to me?'

Madame Cybele stood up and kissed her and said, 'Be very
careful.' Lauren returned the kiss tenderly and felt the young
woman's frail body beneath her winter coat, like a bird's
bones under its feathers.

Usually, she was glad that she seldom saw Madame
Cybele, and she avoided Captain Twilley. And the girls she

saw at parties were too busy hustling to talk. She was alone. She preferred it this way. She regarded herself as a success, both at the agency and at the Institute.

'I've got so much work to do,' she said. But she only went through the motions; she never intended to finish. What was the point? Being an escort had calmed her and made her undemanding at the Institute; and her wide reading had made her a sought-after companion. Now Captain Twilley was polite when he called to give her an appointment, and General Newhouse spoke of extending her Fellowship.

She wrote a paper on the possibilities of a banking crisis precipitated by the overproduction of oil and consequent price-cutting. Her emphasis in the paper was on the economics of Third World countries and their defaulting on debts. The arguments were hers, but Julian had helped her substantiate them by turning over to her all his notes. Afterwards, the General said, 'One word, Miss Slaughter.' It was never 'Mopsy' or 'Doctor'. 'I think that theme is well worth pursuing for publication, but you desperately need documentation.' She remembered this, because within the next half hour a man she had never seen before was kneeling against her and saying, 'Lauren, put this in your mouth.'

The time came for the Study Group to leave for their tour of the Gulf. Julian said, 'We'll miss you.'

'Send me a postcard.'

He misunderstood. He said, 'If it was any other year, I'm sure you'd be going instead of me.'

That was the sort of gentle, dumb remark he made.

Lauren had over three thousand pounds, cash, stuffed in the coffee pot she never used. She had standing invitations in

Kuwait, Bahrain and Qatar. Lord Bulbeck had a regular date with her on Wednesdays and once he had said, 'I don't know what to do about my will. There's my flat, my books, and all my furniture – I shall do whatever you tell me.' She had had a long discussion with the editor of *Arabia Today* ('Pretty much the same as yesterday,' she had said when he told her his paper's name; but she had proven her seriousness by asking about the Sunni-Shia split). 'Anthony J. Pistorino' had wanted to take her to Geneva for a week. Karim was always saying, 'Use my driver.' She believed that she could have anything she wanted.

She said sweetly to Julian, 'One of these days I might get lucky and go. Tell me all about it. But be careful in Kuwait. You'll go in a tight end and come out a wide receiver.'

He inclined his head at her.

'It's a football expression.'

He said, 'Not English football.'

The day Julian and the others left Lauren met a man named Shafique at Half Moon Street – one of Karim's friends, though when she mentioned Karim the man denied that he knew him, and he mysteriously said, 'Who do you work for?'

'Myself,' she said.

One day Ivan Shepherd called the Institute and asked Lauren to dinner. It seemed odd being called 'Lauren' here, but she looked at her appointment book and said yes – tomorrow – and what was the name of his hotel?

He said, 'Ivan Shepherd – don't you remember me?'

'Yes,' she said, 'a long time ago on the subway!'

'Six weeks ago on the tube,' he said. 'How about it?'

'I'm really much too busy these days,' she said; but she wanted to say, *You've got to be joking!*

'Busy doing what?'

Instead of replying she said, 'Hey, did you ever send me anything in the mail?'

'No,' he said, and repeated, 'Busy doing what?'

'Having dinner, actually,' and hung up before he heard her laugh at his presumption, for even if he meant dinner – and he probably didn't – he would be getting free what a grateful man would pay two hundred pounds for.

That was the usual price and they *were* grateful, too, because when she said, 'I want to give you pleasure,' she meant it.

The paradox that particular day, when Ivan Shepherd invited her for dinner – why did men always mention food when they meant fucking? – that same day, Roger, the Assistant Librarian, saw her in the Reference Section and squeezed her breast as if he was honking a horn and she said, 'That *hurt!*' He said, 'If you tell anyone, I'll kill you,' and looked crazily at her.

Also, that same day – this was why she gave up her diary, because there was too much – Karim sent her to visit one of his Kuwaiti friends and the man spent the whole evening drinking tea and earnestly describing desalinization schemes.

It was not sex so much as safety these men looked for. Most of them were wealthy men whom this big foreign city turned into bewildered boys. They knew very little about life in London. They had never heard of Brixton, they thought that a hundred pounds for two in a restaurant was about right, and they were afraid of the dark. They knew nothing.

Lauren said, 'A girlfriend of mine's toilet froze over a few months ago.'

'No.' The man was German. This was at The Inn-on-the-Park. They were in his room watching a pornographic video in which a toilet figured.

He said, 'Your friend was lying to you. It is not cold enough. In Hamburg, yes. In London, no.'

'That's what she said. She never lies.'

'Impossible.'

It made her feel like a heroine; it made her hate her room. She smiled, determined to move out.

'You like it, *ja?*' The German was pleased. He thought she was smiling at the man and the woman and the toilet.

The following Wednesday she told Lord Bulbeck that she was looking for a place to rent in Mayfair. 'Or Queen's Gate?' he said, suggesting that she might want to move in with him; but she was not ready for that. He said he would look around. Some days passed and then, impatiently, she asked the agency to get in touch with him – that was the procedure: a girl could not telephone a client directly. Lord Bulbeck phoned her and said he would gladly find her a flat – and he would pay the rent. 'You don't understand,' she said, but then he rang off saying a motion was being proposed. She tried him twice through the agency, and twice he returned her call: he had one or two leads, he said.

The second time Lauren signalled that she wanted to get in touch with Lord Bulbeck, Madame Cybele said, 'I shouldn't say this to you, but you are being very stupid.'

Lauren said, 'You're right. You shouldn't say that to me.'

And then she had her wish. Karim took her to the flat on

Half Moon Street – to photograph her, she thought. But, no: he toured the three rooms with her. There were cushions and carpets where there had been bare floors, and the room with the clear plastic chairs and the Finnish exercise bike now had plants and bright curtains.

Karim said, 'It's yours. I know the landlord. He needs someone reliable like you. An academic person.'

Of course – because it was people like Roger who treated her like a hooker. *The only person who ever assaulted me and threatened me with murder was an assistant librarian.*

Karim brought her the papers; she signed, she paid, she got the keys and a one-year lease. And she moved into the top floor flat on Half Moon Street, number three.

*

The street itself was nothing – a narrow connection to Piccadilly, the backs of buildings, a small hotel, some black railings, the pale smooth pillars of the Naval and Military Club. But the flat was special, and it made her so happy that when she thought of herself in it, or saw herself in a mirror there (she had always liked the suddenness and the teasing glamour of mirrors: there were five big ones here), she felt important and beautiful and very proud. The first thing she wanted to do at Half Moon Street was call Hugo Van Arkady and say, 'Come over for drinks some evening.' That meant everything. She also wanted to call Lord Bulbeck and treat the good old boy to a free night – it would mean a lot to him. But she couldn't call either man: agency rules. She didn't complain – this isolation as an escort left her free to go to the

[70]

Institute. And in any case one day soon Lord Bulbeck, and probably Van Arkady, would call her and come to the flat and say, 'Ah, you've arrived!'

Half Moon Street was at the very centre of things. She had found the middle of London. And the most remarkable thing about the flat was that though Lauren was often alone in it she was never lonely. That was the test of all property and that was the measure of her happiness on Half Moon Street. It was everything she wanted, and she found her solitude delicious.

She had left Brixton without telling anyone. She had wanted to vanish without a trace – those very words occurred to her. What did Brixton know of Mayfair? This was the London she had always imagined herself in, and as with many people whose fondest wish is granted she felt very healthy, and stronger than ever. She slept soundly. She became very conscientious about her food. Long ago she had banned salt, white sugar, milk, cream or anything with preservatives. Now she banned what she called animal products – no meat at all, not even chicken bouillon cubes. She ate fresh fruit and steamed vegetables, brown rice, lentils, roasted nuts, mushrooms and yogurt. She tried to include half a cup of bran a day. She made stock from potato peel, she drank herbal tea and bottled water, and after a run she had honey on wholemeal toast. Her weakness was for peanut butter. 'I do one of these a week,' she told Rahman – one of Karim's friends – holding up a jar of Harrods' Peanut Butter. Occasionally, she ate fish – poached or broiled, but never fried. 'Like the Hindus say, fish are a kind of sea-vegetable.'

She ran without stopping entirely around the edge of Hyde Park every morning, clockwise from Hyde Park Corner to

Kensington, then north to Bayswater Road and along it to Marble Arch, and down the broad walk parallel to Park Lane. It was seven miles. After a shower – she had four showers a day but only shampooed her hair once – she went to the Institute: library in the mornings, an apple and a piece of cheddar for lunch, and conferences or a seminar in the afternoon. The place was unusually quiet – nearly all the Fellows had gone on the Study Tour to the Gulf, even Brigid, who was supposed to be doing starvation somewhere else, and Fairman the Asia man. Willymot was upstairs counting nuclear warheads, but she never saw him. In the evening after her stretching and a spell on the exercise bike she took agency calls.

It was surprising how many of her dates – she hated Captain Twilley's calling them 'punters' – were interested in eating right. Not Arabs, of course – they stuck to traditional food and were (as well as being generous) the most inflexible and narrow-minded people she had ever known. But Americans, Germans, and all the Scandinavian people liked talking about what Lauren called the dynamics of diet. The sex was predictable – with Karim's friends it was always perfunctory and nearly always bumming; and everyone else wanted to be sucked off. So much for the varieties of sexual experience in Western Civilization! Yet it made life simple and she was glad of that.

But afterwards at the late supper she never ate she often talked about food.

'These tomatoes are very bad for you,' she said. 'They're full of acid. Potato skins are good roughage and loaded with vitamins, and there's a lot of goodness in these snowpeas –

[72]

unless they boiled them. People are always boiling the goodness out of things. But stay away from these dumplings and
that gravy. I always think sausages are just plain destructive.
I'm a salad person –'

She could tell how civilized a man was by his willingness to
listen to reason about his diet. Savages were the real junk-
food freaks, and drinkers and smokers too. She hated
smokers so much she refused to kiss them – it was the only
line she drew – but kissing in the traditional way was the rarest
act she performed. They hugged her and squashed their
hands on her; they pushed her head down. But she didn't
object. Her power was in making them feel powerful, and sex
often made her feel like a ravishing witch, for after they had
come they were small and weak, and they would need her
again to make them strong: the crude magic worked. She
said, 'Fuck my face,' and helped them struggle, and when
they were done she swallowed and said, 'It's good, you know –
it's all protein.'

She considered writing a paper on diet and health, using
Lévi-Strauss's studies of Indian culture and food as a model
for Arabia. She wanted to look at high blood pressure and
heart disease among the super rich in the oil-producing
countries. And what about gastric ulcers and respiratory
ailments – all that drinking and smoking by simple desert
people? But General Newhouse said no. It was not that sort of
institute.

'Unless you plan to publish your findings in *The Lancet* I
suggest you carry on with your study of the recycling of oil
revenues. What a pity you weren't chosen for that Study
Tour.'

[73]

She told Karim that she wanted to talk to Van Arkady. She wanted the victory of his visiting her in Half Moon Street.

Karim said, 'He is very busy. He can't speak to you.'

'Is his bank connected with your embassy in any way?'

'In a way, yes,' he said, challenging her with a smile, 'because I have no embassy.'

'You're being mysterious again.'

'Because you are asking improper questions,' he said. 'Now take your clothes off, my darling. Do you mind?'

'Why should I mind?' And she laughed as she flung them off. Karim was so generous. He had found her this flat, he had given her most of the furniture and that Finnish exercise cycle and a leather chair from Barkers and a Lalique panther made of lead crystal from Harrods. 'But I hate your friend Latif. He's a bully.'

'What does he do?'

Karim was using a large gun-like camera – making a videotape of her pedalling the bike.

She said, 'He spits in my mouth.'

'Lift your knees a bit higher, darling.'

She was not posing but really pedalling for the sake of the film. She said, 'This is great exercise!'

'Stop smiling,' he said. 'What about Rahman.'

'I always confuse him with Raheem.'

'But Raheem is the hungry one.'

'How do you know that?' and turned around to face him.

Karim said, 'Keep pedalling.'

'Yeah,' she said. 'He bites me. Sometimes he leaves marks, and I have to wear my tracksuit to hide them. Some of your friends are real animals.'

'Perhaps only with you,' he said.

She said, 'That's very true. Only I know what they're really like.'

Karim said, 'Go on.'

'Forget it,' she said. 'Rahman gave me some perfume. Tina Farina. In a limited-edition bottle.'

Karim said, 'I don't leave marks,' over the whirr of his camera.

But Lauren was thinking of that terrible German and his toilet movies, and the man who made her put on rubber underwear ('I don't even wear the normal kind!' she complained), and the Spaniard who commanded, 'You must give me a black kiss. Do you know what is a black kiss?'

That was what they were really like: they had small hot secrets.

She said, 'There's no sex anymore.'

Karim had stopped listening. His camera was whirring. He said, 'Pedal harder!'

*

This sex: a virgin could do it and remain a virgin. It was virginal sex, or rather, not sex at all. It was service: she did not feel violated. She was asked to cooperate or perform; to see or be seen. The men groped across her body, some did not touch her at all but merely watched her use her fingers on herself. Often, nothing but her attendance was required – at a banquet or a party. She was once in the same room as the Duke of Edinburgh. The rest was physical, and some of it high school stuff, but it was not sex – not fucking anyhow –

and though it frequently confused her it left her feeling pure. Now she understood Madame Cybele's distraction, and those bruises on the young woman's white skin.

6

When a man asked for more time all he wanted was time. At dinner he might say, 'I want you for breakfast, too,' but he would then spend the rest of the night snoring beside her in his king-sized bed, or else showing her off to his friends – towing her in and out of rooms for them to admire. So greedy, so eager, so puny! Most of them had nothing but money, which seemed to Lauren like the cruellest form of destitution. They overreached themselves, these men, in sex as in their business lives. Their loneliness made them unreasonable. But usually they just submerged themselves in sleep.

All that was required of her was tact – don't mention the uneaten meal, the sudden sleep, the unused and useless portion of the jeroboam of champagne: not a word about the hopeless fumble and apology, that bump in the night: 'Sorry, I don't think – oh, never mind –' She wanted to say, 'You don't have to apologize, darling.' They were demanding by nature, but in the circumstances in which she saw them they were children. She wanted to say: *Your eyes are bigger than your – et cetera!* They made her feel like third helpings. And there she lay until they woke up blinking at her pretty face and honey-blonde hair.

Often they wanted no more than her companionship. One man, a superstitious Portuguese – banking – spent hours showing her his good-luck charms, and they included a

shrunken head – a hard hairy prune with sewn-up lips. A man
from Needles, California, who was working on an oil rig in the
North Sea had a gold belt buckle engraved *If You Ain't Oilfield
You Ain't Shit*. With such men it wasn't sex. It was that they
did not want to be left alone and lonesome in this wet
winter-dark city. Sometimes it was just like a sink.

This particular man asked for a weekend. He said his name
was Guy, and Lauren knew he wasn't lying – Guy was not the
kind of name you made up.

'What did you have in mind?'

Once a man had said: *What kind of knickers* –?

'Nothing special,' Guy said.

For a weekend! But really it was just the sort of vagueness
she expected for this length of time. He was like the rest of
them, except that he was being honest.

She said, 'A weekend's a long time.'

'In the country it passes quite quickly,' he said. He
sounded cute and nervous. 'We'll be staying with friends. It's
all arranged.'

He picked her up late Friday afternoon at the Institute in
his Triumph. He was young, about twenty-eight – but some
of these English people could look much older than they
were, wearing incredibly ugly clothes and with terrible posture, and there were thirty-year-olds in London who had grey
hair. Guy was surprisingly good-looking and probably played
tennis – he certainly didn't smoke. He walked on the balls of
his feet in a tennis-player's way. Now Lauren was glad it was
going to be a weekend.

The agency fee for this was three hundred pounds. Lauren
considered asking only another three hundred, she liked him

[78]

so much, but she didn't want him to think she was a hooker, so she decided on an even thousand. She kept the price to herself for the moment.

He said, 'I love finishing work on a Friday and leaving London. It's like breaking out of jail.'

He drove too fast – over seventy: the English were so childish about speed, and the other Europeans were worse, French and Italians especially. But at least he kept both hands on the wheel.

They were on the Great West Road and had now passed the suburbs of semi-detached houses, the vegetable fields farther on, the airport. Now it was dark, and just the occasional scatter of lighted windows far off the road indicated a town or a village. Now and then a sign saying *Wales* or *Oxford* flew at them from the darkness ahead.

His dog woke up and began barking. Lauren had taken the thing for a hairy blanket in the jump seat. She felt his damp nose at the back of her ear and something else against her hair – perhaps his jowls or his flapping tongue. He stopped barking, he slurped at the side of her head; and she smiled, remembering much worse men.

Guy said, 'Get down, you stupid dog!' and the animal retreated.

'He doesn't bother me,' Lauren said.

'He thinks he's a person, that's his problem. He's really neurotic. He prevents me from having anything like a worth-while relationship with anyone else. He gets jealous.'

Lauren was enjoying the solitary pleasure of smiling in the dark. She had not been this happy for months. Yes, she thought. They never had animals, and they were never so young, and never so relaxed. Guy was an unusual fellow. He wasn't shifty or apologetic. I could even stand the dog, she thought. She saw herself walking the beast in Hyde Park on Sunday mornings and buying newspapers at the corner and bringing them back to Guy. He wasn't like any of the others. This weekend was going to be fun.

'What's his name?'

'Him? Shmuel.'

'What's it mean?'

'It means he's a special sort of mutt, like me.'

Lauren said, 'I think you are pretty special.' When he laughed at this she added, 'I think I am, too,' and he stopped laughing.

Answering one of her direct questions, Guy said that he worked at a merchant bank. He startled Lauren by saying, 'I have a rather lowly position at the moment, but if I get a transfer I'll move up a few grades. I've put in for Hong Kong.'

Lauren said, 'There's much more money in the Gulf. Doha, for example, would be perfect. I've been to Hong Kong – so I know. The Gulf is my field now.'

Guy said, 'The Gulf might be awkward for me.'

'Not if you want to do business,' she said. 'You should see the profiles of some of these Gulf banks. Mega-bucks!' There was not much light on Guy's face, but he seemed to be smiling and nodding in agreement. She said, 'I bet we've got a lot in common.'

Why didn't he say something?

She said, 'We could meet there. It might be fun travelling together.'

He smiled again, but was staring straight ahead at the

empty road. Finally he said softly, 'I'm sure you know much more than I do about the Gulf.'

'Want to know a secret?' Lauren said, but she had already started to laugh. 'I don't know shit about the Gulf! I chose it because it's the opposite of China – that was my husband's big thing. But the Gulf – God, I don't know the difference between emirates and interest rates, and I'm supposed to be able to talk Gulf economics! Hey, I'm just sucking my thumb.'

Guy's expression did not change. He was still smiling in a studious way at the tunnel his headlights made on the road ahead. Lauren wondered whether she was boring him.

She said, 'I don't know why I told you that,' and frowned. 'Maybe it's because I've never told anyone else.'

He said, 'You've got a husband.'

'*Had* a husband.' He had missed the point – seized on the most unimportant detail.

'And China!' he said.

He really had missed the point by a mile. She said, 'You've never been there or else you wouldn't be so wild about Hong Kong. China's just boring and depressing, but Hong Kong is worse in a different way – if it was human you'd say it was tasteless, spoiled, overweight and had high blood pressure. When the lease expires in 1997 the PRC is going to take over and kick the shit out of it. People are already leaving – and you want to go there!'

He said, 'You know these places intimately, of course.'

'Sure. My Chinese work got me the Hemisphere fellowship.'

'What about your escort work?'

'It's not work.'

He said nothing. It was an English habit not to hit the ball back. You sometimes had to serve again and again.

'I'm flexible,' she said.

He kept driving.

'I can fit anything in,' she said.

Maybe he hated himself for being with her.

'I live alone, so most of my evenings are free.'

He said, 'So you're not seeing anyone at the moment.'

She laughed. 'I'm seeing a lot of people! But not steadily. Do you know what I mean by a sex-partner?'

'Approximately. Have you got one?'

'Not at the moment.'

'And yet,' Guy said, 'something tells me you've got your hands full.'

She said, 'You'd be surprised how much I can handle.'

He chose not to reply – well, what could he say? And he was concentrating on his driving. They drove off the motorway onto a dark twisting road, walled by thick hedges which showed in the headlights.

Lauren meanwhile had been reflecting in a hopeful way, and now her mind was made up. She said, 'I'm sure it would work out.'

'Sorry?'

'You and me,' she said. 'In the Gulf. Doha, for example. A kind of working vacation at first. I'm sure we've both got a lot of contacts there. We could just play it by ear and share expenses – see how we get along. It might be fun.'

He said, 'I put in for Hong Kong, but even if I tried to get a transfer to the Gulf it might not go through for another year.'

He sniggered in a self-deprecating way and added, 'I don't fancy my chances.'

'You'd get it easily!'

'You don't know a thing about me,' he said, almost sternly.

Then Lauren realized that she had gone too far, planned too much – she was always skipping ahead. But she had been dealing with rich successful men; she wasn't used to young struggling executives who called themselves 'middle management' and were anxious for a one-rung promotion.

'It's not far,' Guy said. 'Just a few more miles.'

Lauren said, 'You don't have to apologize, darling.'

*

He had been there before – she could tell by the way he raced up the driveway, taking the two curves fast and scattering pebbles as he braked before the stone canopy at the front door. Lauren was saying 'Hi!' to the old man approaching the car, but Guy said nothing, only gave the man the key to his boot, and then Lauren realized she was warmly greeting the butler – the servant anyhow – babbling at him. She was embarrassed, but decided to make a democratic virtue of the gaffe and kept talking to the old man as he heaved the bags at the door.

She sensed something like hostility in the man – fear and anger – he was trying to drive her off and save himself, because how could he explain to his employer – the woman who was walking slowly towards Lauren – that this American girl had insisted on chatting with him?

'Guy!' the woman cried and lifted her hands to his face.

She was tall and bony and sure of herself. She wore a shapeless grey suit and had white streaks in her hair. But Lauren saw that she was not more than thirty-five or so – she had young skin and lovely hands.

'And this is your young lady,' the woman said, turning to Lauren. 'You must be the lovely Julia.'

'I'm not,' Lauren said. 'Does this mean I have to go back home?'

Guy said, 'Maura, this is –'

'Dr Slaughter,' Lauren said, putting her hand out. 'But you can call me Lauren.'

The woman did not take her hand, and so Lauren stood there feeling like someone who had just dropped something.

Maura said, 'I'd much rather call you Dr Slaughter.'

Lauren said, 'If it'll make you feel better.'

Maura was still speaking. 'Like someone in Trollope.'

They had been walking quickly as they spoke and were now past the hall and approaching a long room where two men and another woman were sitting before a fireplace. The men got to their feet as Maura entered with Guy and Lauren.

'I always like a little Trollope in bed before I go to sleep,' one of the men said and smiled at Lauren.

'So does Sam,' the other man said.

'Wasn't it Harold Macmillan who said that?'

'Surely it was Lennox Berkeley?'

Lauren saw that each person in the room was sneaking glances at her and, as they knew Guy, probably sizing her up. Was she good for him? Were they serious? Did she have anything to offer? Did she have a nice figure? You silly fucks, she thought.

[84]

The other woman, introduced to her as Sidney, asked – apropos of what? – 'Are you interested in music, Dr Slaughter?'

She said, 'I like playing the mouth organ.'

'Do you know English music?'

'I think it's tremendously underrated – particularly in America,' Lauren said.

'There!' Maura said.

'The Stranglers are way ahead of their time,' Lauren said. 'They're practically geniuses.'

'You're a very brave girl.' Was that man smiling?

Sidney said, 'I'm not familiar with the Stranglers, I'm afraid.'

' "Shah-Shah a Go-Go"? "Baroque Bordello"? "Walking on the beaches, looking at the peaches"? "Rattus Norvegicus"?'

Lauren stared at them as she spoke.

'Slaughter,' the woman named Sidney said in a thoughtful way. 'Don't I know your father from Nairobi?'

Maura said, 'I'll show you upstairs.'

They had separate rooms, she and Guy, and not even adjoining ones.

Lauren said, 'Is this going to work out?'

'Perfectly.'

'You'll need a map!'

But she wanted to say, *I hope these people aren't good friends of yours, because I sort of hate them.* Instead she said nothing; she liked Guy too much to embarrass him. She saw that he was a few years younger than she and she wanted him more: *My young husband . . .*

She knew they were trying to mock her, but she did not know whether they were succeeding – and that was maddening. They were certainly telling private jokes, which was a way of ignoring her; but were they ridiculing her?

'Americans put such extraordinary things on their feet,' Maura said, after Lauren and Guy returned to the long room.

They kept saying things like that. But this time Lauren decided not to let it pass.

She said, 'Every time I see an Englishman I think, "What's that stuff on his head?" '

She felt their gaze on her.

She said, 'And it's usually hair.'

Alan – Maura's husband – said, 'You're new in London, I take it.'

'Sort of. I could have had Peking, but I'd been there before. I figured I'd try London and if it didn't work out I'd look at my options.'

'I understand,' Maura said. 'She said to herself, "I'll suck it and see." That's very American.'

Did they know something?

Alan said, 'I can't think what's keeping Sam.'

Guy said, 'He's probably speaking. You know Sam.'

'Yes,' the woman named Sidney said. 'He's a very passionate man in actual fact, isn't he?'

'On certain subjects,' Guy said.

More private jokes, Lauren thought: mock the guest by keeping her in the dark. She had an urge to say: *There was a girl named Roberta Wiljanen at my school who had six toes –*

'Your young lady must be ravenous.'

No, just bored stiff – and she hated to be spoken about in

[86]

the third person: the big English thing. She said, 'I'm not hungry at all. I had an apple, some walnuts and plain yogurt just before I left London.'

Maura, suspecting, looked annoyed.

'Vegetarian,' Lauren said, and beamed.

She had kicked off her shoes. They looked at her feet.

Maura said, 'There's roast beef for dinner.'

'I'll just have a little salad.'

'Perhaps we can organize an omelette for you.'

Lauren let disgust flicker across her face. 'In some ways eggs are worse than meat.'

'Now I never knew that!' the second man said. His name was George – 'Geo', the others called him. He had seemed fascinated by what Lauren had said, but it was all show. He turned abruptly to Maura and said, 'Next week at this time you'll be in Les Houches.'

'Aren't you going this year?'

'Been,' he said. 'But we're through with Chamonix.' He smacked his lips and said, 'Val d'Isère. Fabulous. Powder. Three thousand metres. Scared Sidney rigid.'

Guy said, 'I was at Mégève over Christmas.'

'Was it fabulous?' Maura asked. 'I've heard Mégève's heaven.'

Guy said, 'I think I marginally prefer Klosters. Greta Garbo lives there, but so what?'

They were off, they kept talking, and they had turned their backs on Lauren. No one addressed a word to her, and it took her some minutes of listening to work out that they were talking about skiing. From this conversation she was totally excluded – she wondered whether it had something to do with her having blurted out that she was a vegetarian. God, she had enjoyed telling them that. It always wrong-footed a hostess when you saved that for the last minute.

She hated this skiing business – people they knew, places they'd been, heaven, fabulous, exquisite food. It was all incredibly boring, just a recitation of names, because how could you discuss skiing except to say that one place was good and another was lousy? It was stupid and the proof was would anyone talk this way about swimming? And it was the same kind of thing.

But the worst of it was that Lauren had never been skiing.

'I'm told that Les Arcs is really superb. We didn't book in time. You fly to Geneva and take a coach. The pistes run right up to the hotel apparently.'

Should she say that she had skiied but had given it up after a serious leg injury; or still skiied every year in Aspen – yes, we have lots of skiing right in Colorado; or should she mock the whole idea of it and say that it was like talking about swimming? But no one asked her. The conversation did not come her way. She didn't count. And when Guy became solicitous and asked her in a whisper whether he could get her another glass of Malvern water, she began to dislike him and to wish that she had never come.

They're really and truly awful, she thought, and she grew a little sentimental thinking about the busy breathless man she would be with tonight; she thought of Karim, and of Lord Bulbeck, and their loneliness. She had liked Guy on his own, and she hoped it would be like that again upstairs.

'I much prefer the food at the French resorts.'

They were still talking about skiing!

'Bumpy gave me a new pair of boots for Christmas,' Alan said.

'I got a really chic anorak,' Sidney said. 'And matching salopettes.'

Anorak? Salopettes? Lauren wanted to laugh at them.

Perhaps they noticed her smiling, because Maura said, 'Do you ski?'

'Periodically.'

Then an alert listening look brightened Maura's face. Lauren had seen that look before on other people – it was a house-owner hearing the sound of someone in the driveway. It was inaudible to everyone else; you had to own the house to hear it.

'That must be Sam.'

Maura went into the hallway and after a suspended silence she shouted at her guest and there was a commotion – stamping feet, the banging of a suitcase, a loud kiss, a slammed door.

'He's here –'

And now the men were calling across the long room, and bantering, 'We'd just about given you up, Sam,' because the guest was so late, and in this chatter Guy said, 'Hello, uncle.'

Lauren was thinking: Another one. And since they all pretended to be old-fashioned here she decided to keep her back turned and go on toasting her toes until they got around to introducing her. She sat with the cat on her lap, thinking about skiing, how she had never gone. But you couldn't do everything.

Now the guest was in the room, treading the carpet.

Guy smiled with a kind of insistence at Lauren – he wanted her to get up and greet his uncle. His uncle! England was all relatives!

'And this is Dr Slaughter,' Maura was saying. 'She is rather preoccupied at the moment with our cat, Rudy. Perhaps she is a vet? Dr Slaughter, I'd like you to meet Lord Bulbeck.'

She turned quickly and saw that he was smiling. He shook her hand and said, 'Pleased to meet you, my dear.'

She could not see either affection or anger in his smile, and feeling off balance she looked for Guy. He was talking with Sidney, the younger of the two women, who was so self-assured with her big knockers, pretending she didn't see them swinging. Guy looked interested and responsive, that flirtatious energy, that nervous thirst, and Sidney was enjoying his discomfort and turning her headlights on him. Guy was different now from the circumspect young man who had driven her up from London. If Lord Bulbeck had not been there she would have taken Guy aside and whispered, 'I'm going to sneak into your room upstairs and eat you.'

But Lord Bulbeck was still smiling vaguely at her, with a kind of forced politeness. And, when Maura told him she was off to Les Houches, he said, 'I know it's not an originoo thought, but the French have no principoos.'

'That was a very flattering profile of you in *The Times* last week,' Geo said.

'I don't find it flattering when journalists refer to my nose as bowbus.'

'I meant your part in those Middle East peace talks.'

'I'm just an errand boy,' Lord Bulbeck said.

He had the floor. When he spoke everyone listened.

He said, 'It's a horriboo errand.'

Lauren loved the way he talked, his little bubble-blower's mouth puckered under his fat nose: *originoo . . . principoo . . . bowbus . . . horriboo.* And she was sorry that he was probably mad at her for finding her here with someone else. But that was tough luck for him: everyone paid, which was why she was free.

The hostess seated Lord Bulbeck next to herself and separated Lauren from Guy, so that Lauren was stuck with Geo, the middle-aged man who said, 'I came to skiing rather late,' and then began boasting, in his English way, at what frightful risks he took and how bad he was.

For Lauren, all dinners were very long: it was her being a vegetarian that made this so – she knew; and as a non-drinker she found most parties interminable. Her only diversion was in seeing how carnivores and boozers underwent a personality change as they crammed the junk into their mouths. Meat-eaters grew tired in an animalistic way – did they know how long it took flesh to be digested? – and drinkers just got crazier. Now, after the meal, everyone was clumsier and louder, sort of stumbling like squinting zoo monkeys after their feed. Lauren almost ran from the dining room when it was over – she hadn't exercised all day: that was the trouble – but Lord Bulbeck headed her off, and before the others overtook them he said, 'You're looking well.'

'I hope you're not mad,' she said. 'I never met these people before. I came with Guy.'

'Of course –'

'You probably want to kill me. But I didn't know he was your nephew.'

[91]

'If he wasn't you wouldn't be here,' Lord Bulbeck said. 'And neither would I.'

'I don't get it.'

'I'll explain everything later,' he said. 'Upstairs.'

She said, 'I'm a fellow at the Hemisphere Institute,' because the others had entered the room.

He said, 'You're a lovely fellow!'

But upstairs, after midnight, Lord Bulbeck did not explain anything. He came to her room and in his big soft funny-uncle way he held her and told her how beautiful she was.

She said, 'So it was a trap.'

'I know all about traps,' he said. 'People try to trap me often enough.'

'But it's a pretty roundabout way of getting me into bed,' she said.

'Very roundabout, very safe.'

She said, 'Think how safe it would be in France.'

'Frants,' he said. So he found her pronunciation funny, too!

She said, 'I want to go skiing, Sam.'

'Anything you want, ducky, but please don't call me Sam at breakfast.'

It was a perfect weekend. She was two people, and it worked so well she had at times glimpses of a third – the person she believed in and trusted. On Sunday evening she drove back to London with Guy, and neither said a single word.

7

They had travelled in the same plane to Geneva; but in different sections – Lord Bulbeck flew under the name Green in First Class and Lauren was Mopsy Fairlight (it was an old passport) in Tourist. They went through Customs at the same time; but Lord Bulbeck was waved along by an official and he was picked up by a Mercedes flying a United Nations flag, while Lauren took a taxi. They were both staying at the Holiday Inn, but in separate rooms. And yet at midnight they were together – in his room – and again he marvelled at her beauty.

'You Americans are so big and healthy.' He spoke with gratitude and even humility. He said, 'I'm so lucky to know you. I feel puny and old.'

'That's why you don't want us to be seen together.'

'That's not the principoo reason.'

She laughed hard, and she laughed again when he said the word, 'genitoos'.

'You'll be real healthy after the skiing,' she said.

'We shall see.'

That was their first night in Geneva, which seemed to her an uglier and duller place than shoreline Chicago, which it somewhat resembled – Chicago with mountains. Lord Bulbeck told her that his committee would keep him there for a few days and that he would follow her to the resort.

'You're going tomorrow,' he said. 'Get an early start. The car's coming for you at eight. It's a four-hour drive to Bourg St Maurice, and I'm told the hotel is on an impossiboo road at 1,800 metres.'

'You have to promise on the Bible to be there.'

'The Byboo is not my book,' he said. 'But I promise.'

Lauren left him in the dark early morning and went to her room to pack. The driver was young and very silent, but she saw his eyes in the rear-view mirror; and she was reminded of a taxi driver in London, who took her back to Brixton and demanded nine pounds because it was after midnight, and she had said, 'Come upstairs – wouldn't you rather be paid there?' and she had done him in a few minutes and sent him down exhausted. That was fun, but that was before. She thought: I'll only do it for fun again, and if I want it.

They crossed drearily into France on wet gritty streets which continued for miles, and then to Annecy where the snow was coated with a black lacework of soot. The lake was an improvement, and soon the light was better and they were in sight of high mountains, and an hour later they were climbing them. They made their way along the sides of valleys, the road like a gutter hacked across the steepness. There was snow everywhere and vast knobbed icicles hung from cliffs and from the glacial sluices in the crevasses between the valleys.

Beneath the rising road was a loud, almost demented-sounding river battering greeny boulders and crashing along the deep stone trough, uselessly shoving at the walls. The mountains had no peaks: they penetrated a ceiling of cloud that was like sky-stuffing and that in places had slipped sideways to reveal in torn holes sky the colour of tropical water – aquamarine that seemed as pure and soft as a harmless gas. She thought that oxygen must look like that. The snow by the roadside was pushed into precipitous heaps, and nearer Bourg St Maurice what people she saw were either skiers or peasants – wearing absurdly bright colours and ridiculous hats, or else dark heavy coats and black boots.

The last ten miles to the high slopes of Les Arcs were a twisting ascent in which Lauren began to imagine herself upraised on a skyhook that made everything around her vanish – the cliffs, the ice, the pines, even the road – everything but the car in which she sat. The car seemed to tremble on an air current. Her ears crackled like static. She was in empty space and only she was real; but no – it was the whiteness of the snow.

The next day was sunny and bright, and she was amazed that at this altitude, among all this snow, she was comfortable and not even cold. She left her ski suit unzipped. She was in a beginners' class, on rented skis, very short ones; the resort was famous for this method.

'Are you alone?' It was an American woman sitting beside her in the chairlift. Lauren had taken her for a German – she had German eyes: ice-blue, humourless, lovely.

Lauren said, 'At the moment.'

'I was just wondering if you had a partner – a husband or a friend.'

'I have both,' Lauren said. 'Periodically.'

'I like you!' the woman said. 'My husband's a great skier, but he's so competitive! He's at the Aiguille Rouge today.

What's that – ten thousand feet? He wants to get dropped out of a helicopter somewhere around Mon Blong. I got sick of staying in Vence, that's where we live, he's with GE. But I hate being a beginner. I was watching you stumble up to this lift and I thought: She's just as bad as me. I'm Ellen.'

She had said too much; she had spoiled it, so all Lauren said was, 'How big is the class?'

'Just the five of us from last week, and you, and that new guy.' Ellen was pointing her ski poles at the man in the swinging chair in front of them – his head made smooth and compact by a snugly-fitting ski hat.

'Here we are,' Lauren said, seeing the man glide away from his chair at the top of the lift.

'Don't knock me over,' Ellen said, and just as they arrived she panicked, shoved Lauren sideways and then tripped her.

Lauren was emptying the snow from the inside of her gloves when Ellen hobbled over to her. But, instead of apologizing she said, 'Those chairlifts are hell!'

Lauren said, 'I know how to fall.'

But Ellen was looking at the new student. 'I'm probably prejudiced but I have to laugh when I see blacks on skis. He's probably a Hindu or something. Doesn't he look a little out of place?'

Lauren said 'I've seen them in all sorts of places', and there was an edge in her voice that did not invite reply from the women.

Stumbling and slipping, falling in ways that looked comic but that were painful and embarrassing, the class – growing more frightened and less determined as it fell – zigzagged to the foot of the long slope. The instructor, a woman with red

[96]

peeling cheeks and a faded blue ski jacket, stamped her skis and muttered in French. 'No, no, no,' she said contemptuously as one by one each person in the class fell, negotiating a little half-hidden hump of snow.

Later in the morning, Lauren found herself next to the newcomer in the chairlift. She had wanted that, but had he helped? He was very calm, hardly looking at her.

'I'm studying the Arab world,' she said. 'Where are you from?'

He said, 'The Arab world,' and smiled. 'But my business takes me all over. My parent company is based in London.'

Why was it that only Arabs and Indians used expressions like 'parent company'?

She said, 'We must have an awful lot in common.'

'Then we should have lunch.'

'I'm just going to have an apple in my room.'

He said nothing. They were arriving at the top of the lift. They struggled off without falling and shuffled to where the class was waiting.

'Do you have two apples?' he said.

At noon, he knocked on her door carrying a large basket of fruit wrapped in cellophane and ribbon. He had a yard of French bread and a small wheel of Camembert and two bottles of wine. Typical Arab overkill: he could have brought one apple. But she was getting to like the needless gesture and found it a comfort.

She said, 'I don't drink, but I sure do like bananas,' and removed one from the basket and peeled in a slow unzipping way, with her teeth.

They sat by the window and stared at the luminous blue

snow and the white sky and the spindly black pines. Now it looked very cold outside.

Lauren said, 'I should tell you, I'm alone at the moment, but I'm waiting for someone.'

The man nodded; had he seen something outside?

'My father,' she said.

'We'd better hurry,' he said, and touched her, though he was still peering outside.

'We've got plenty of time.' She began wriggling out of her ski suit. 'I hate wearing all these clothes.'

They missed the afternoon class, and when they awoke from the short deep sleep – was it the sex or the altitude? – it was snowing. The flakes were large and loose, as big as fur balls, and swaying past the yellow lamps that lined the buried path beside the hotel.

His name was Sonny, but probably not, and he might have been from Syria – he was very vague and he also mumbled when he seemed unwilling to reply. She did not want to know more: there was always a commitment in asking questions and expecting replies, and she knew she often became un- reasonably eager when she heard things like 'I'm looking for someone to run my Qatar operation.'

He was handsome – watchful, appreciative, very strong. He made love to her in an old-fashioned impaling way – it had been months since a man had done that, and he surprised her by chafing her into orgasm. Then it was like levitation, a mid-air feeling, and all her nerves singing – energy in her fingers and toes – until the orgasm shook and scorched her and she fell back to earth and began to cry. She tasted her tears; she was proud of them; she gave herself to them and

[98]

faked them a little more until Sonny was pleased and frightened.

'This has never happened to me before,' she said.

'Some women never have one.'

'I mean, the crying,' and she let the tears dry on her cheeks.

After that they skipped most of the classes. She used the sauna and the exercise cycle in the hotel's health club, and Sonny fed francs into the electronic games in the resort's game room. Lauren liked watching him play the idiotic video games, seeing him amaze the young French boys with the rattle of his enormous scores. 'They call this "Frogger" in England, but here it is called "Jumper".' He played that croaking one reluctantly. He preferred the high-speed rocket chases and machine-gun games that were full of asteroids and explosives.

It seemed a just revenge on the skiers, who were either experts or incompetents. People came for one week to learn how to ski! Then they came next year for another week! It was exhausting, dangerous, expensive and – Lauren thought – pure show-off. Did anyone ever ski alone? The idea was to have someone watching you do it better than they could. Something in the whole ski thing reminded Lauren of details she had heard about health spas a hundred years ago – immersion cures and colonic irrigation and 'taking the waters' and generally going to a lot of trouble in order to justify eating well and meeting people and getting laid at a high altitude.

The first two days she forgot about everything except meeting Sonny and making love. This was the kind of sex she had been denied in London. She needed him for it; she loved it, she ached. It was certainly better for you than skiing. It was always in her room, and he always gave her time to herself. He had a lot of sense for an Arab: he cared about her pleasure.

'What about your father?' he said on the morning of the third day.

'My father –' She looked pained: agony. Her father was dead.

Then she remembered.

'I'd better call him.'

It took her the whole morning to get a line, and when she reached the Holiday Inn in Geneva the line was bad. 'Speak louder,' the operator said, but Lauren was already shouting. She screamed her name, she spelled Lord Bulbeck's, and then hung up, hoping the operator was deafened by the crash of the receiver – but they never heard more than a click, did they?

The phone call worked. That evening there was a telegram: REGRET UNABLE TO MEET YOU. WILL RING YOU ON RETURN TO LONDON. No signature – what a cautious man! – but she knew who it was from.

Sonny was playing 'Moon Landing' in the game room, working a jolting vehicle and firing with it at looming monsters. A crowd of French children had gathered around him and looked very impressed.

'He's not coming.' She didn't say 'my father' – it gave her the creeps to say the word now.

Sonny said, 'I've earned five credits. That's a free game.'

'You know where I'll be, darling.' She went to the hotel to exercise and change. She liked this life here: she wanted more of it – not the skiing, but everything else.

She waited until ten o'clock. Her certainty and her antici-
pated pleasure made her patient. But just after ten she craved
an orange and called Sonny's room to remind him to bring
some. The phone was dead. She dressed and went looking for
him. His room was locked. He was not in the game room. On
a whim she asked at the front desk.

'He checked out two hours ago. He is gone.'

Why did the French seem to take such pleasure in giving a
person bad news?

*

She went back to London and at last, after an unexplained
two weeks without seeing her, Lord Bulbeck phoned her at
Half Moon Street and said he wanted to take her to a play. It
was a West End revival of *A Streetcar Named Desire*, but she
insisted on leaving at the intermission.

She said, 'Tennessee Williams would hate my guts. But it's
a phony play, so that doesn't matter. Only a fairy could have
written that play and gotten everything wrong.'

Lord Bulbeck said, 'I can't imagine anyone hating you.'

'I'm the sort of healthy open-minded girl that people used
to call a nymphomaniac,' she said.

They went to the Savoy Restaurant. Lord Bulbeck asked to
be seated in a corner, away from the view of the Thames.
Lauren had two appetizers and nothing else. Lord Bulbeck
had smoked buckling, and then steak and grouse pie, and
finally sherry trifle.

'You're killing yourself,' Lauren said.

Lord Bulbeck wiped his mouth and ordered a schooner of

port. He said, 'I missed your dire warnings. And I missed other things.'

'I thought you'd forgotten about me. You never came skiing. It was fun.'

'I had to return suddenly to London.'

'You still haven't visited me here!'

Lord Bulbeck said, 'But you moved to a new place.'

'That's just it. I wanted you to see it.'

He said, 'I wonder if it's safe.'

'Everyone worries about me!' Lauren said. 'I can take care of myself!'

'I meant me,' Lord Bulbeck said. 'I have to be very careful you see.'

He was eating the sherry trifle still. His conversation was always full of maddening pauses when he was eating.

'It's my views.' He chewed and swallowed. 'I'm on a certain council – I'm chairman. Improbable as it may seem,' and he chewed and swallowed again, 'some people have threatened me with trouble.'

As always she was fascinated and distracted by his pronunciation. He said 'sherry tryfoo' and 'cownsoo' and 'improbaboo' and 'peepoo' and 'truboo'. But what was he talking about? She wondered whether it was an upper-class accent, and she suspected that it wasn't. But it was lovely in its way. Why was the poor man looking so serious?

'– getting used to peroo,' he was saying.

Could that be *peril*?

Now he changed the subject, perhaps because she had been so interested in his accent that she had not said a word. He said, 'I suppose you've been seeing other men?'

[102]

'Seeing them, yes.'

'I imagine they just want to get you into bed.'

'*Bed*?' she said. 'Bed? I haven't been in bed with anyone for weeks. You're the only man I go to bed with.'

Lord Bulbeck said, 'You're joking, of course.'

'I'm serious,' she said. 'On a table, on a chair, on an exercise bike, in the bathroom – yes. But not in a bed.'

'How is it to make love on an exercise bike?'

Lauren said, 'He was taking pictures of my thing.'

'And a bathroom,' Lord Bulbeck said, making a face. He was hardly listening. Sex was so often a completely private set of fantasies.

'We weren't making love,' Lauren said. 'He was shaving me.'

Lord Bulbeck said, 'But not shagging you.'

'No. But last week I came close. I've got this other guy who takes me out. He's an American engineer, working on weather satellite technology. He's got this girlfriend, Debbie. She's from Scotland and she's got this really neat accent. Usually we go to his place and he puts on a video. It's always something dykey. Then we watch it and he gets Debbie and me to start kissing. I mean, we really make out. Is that what shagging is?'

Lord Bulbeck had become very intent. He swallowed, concentrating hard, and said, 'Then what happens?'

'Then he fucks Debbie while I watch and then we all go out to dinner,' Lauren said. 'But I never eat anything except salad. I'm a salad person.'

'Go on about the other thing,' Lord Bulbeck said.

What *other thing*? she thought. She said, 'Well, you men-

[103]

tioned bed, but there isn't much of that. Men don't want a woman. They want an object. I mean literally. "Stand very still," they say. They want me to be a pillow or a chair or a table or a pet rabbit. They want me to be a *thing*. It's ridiculous!'

Lord Bulbeck said, 'I'd like to go to your flat with you right now and take you to bed.'

'Yes, yes,' she said. 'That'll be a change.'

'I'm quite in the mood,' he said. He paid the bill and they left the restaurant.

She said, 'It's good for you to leave the rest of that dessert. And coffee is just horrible.'

They went to Half Moon Street. Lord Bulbeck went into each room, sniffing, touching, looking out of the windows. 'There's the famous exercise bike,' he said. He reminded her of a detective searching for clues, and when he was satisfied that there were none he undressed with his usual care, one cuff button then the other, and shaking each leg out of his trousers, and piling everything onto a chair. It was the clear plastic chair. She had not told him about that – how she pressed herself against it for Karim.

She wanted to say, 'Sex isn't sex – at least, that isn't.' It was rarified and distant and private, the small corners of private fantasies. Now she and Lord Bulbeck were in her bed at Half Moon Street for the first time, and he was stroking her slowly: like a lover, she thought. That was it – the men were not lovers. Most of them did not even touch her. She found it impossible to enter the feelings of these men. She tried: she wanted to share that thrill and to know that satisfaction. But there was only the ritual, the solitary orgasm, and no satisfaction. They probably didn't have any feelings at all. Sonny the great lover had just ditched her!

'Did I hurt you?' she said.

'A littoo,' Lord Bulbeck said. 'Why?'

'You moved!'

But she was joking, because he lay beside her, exhausted, looking mugged.

Later, she said, 'I'm really glad you finally came here. This flat is special.' She felt his hand on her: he had tried hard to please her. She said, 'And you're special.' But she could not use the word lover for someone with so many secrets.

8

When Karim said, 'There is someone I want you to meet,' she was prepared for anything. It was a silent man with a suitcase. The suitcase made her reflective. The ones who used props always seemed a little unsteady emotionally – even Karim and his camera, the way he poked the thing at her. And as with some of the others Karim insisted that she take this man to Half Moon Street.

That day, Lauren had agreed to read a paper at the Thursday seminar which covered topics of current interest – General Newhouse called the papers 'backgrounders'. Lauren did not have a paper, nor had she submitted any work to the Fellowship Committee. She gathered newspaper clippings and wire service reports, and she filed and cross-referenced them with the financial analyses – anything to do with oil revenue investments. But all revenue was oil revenue! She wished she had never begun the project – China would have been easier, food would have been more fun; but she would still have had to face those scraps of paper and those fat files. She could gather material but she could not write.

Writing was so hard. It was not just setting down your thoughts or putting those clippings into a narrative, but more like learning how to think and then teaching yourself to write. It was not just hard – it was impossible for her. Her hand stiffened on her keyboard after the first *bop-bop-bop*.

She thought: I should get one of these word-processors.

The Institute had a computer, with a telescreen and a printer. She sat at it with a stack of notes. *Chk-chk.* And then, *chk-chk-chk.* But it didn't think. It was a glorified typewriter. There was a game they played every Fourth of July on the courthouse lawn in Turkey Hollow – the peanut race. You pushed a peanut with your nose, six feet to the Civil War Memorial. That's what writing was; and she looked at her notes: this is my peanut.

And the task was much larger and sometimes when she was trying to write, it was as if she were trying to invent the written word – like originating language itself. Impossible. And what about spending every night with those men? She was strong, but she did not have time enough to write and also live her other life.

She did not write a seminar paper, but instead spoke from her notes. Suspecting that the others would think she was frivolous if she wore a dress – it was almost April but very sunny, and warm enough for her Laura Ashley pinafore – she decided on her tweed jacket and severe blouse and grey flat-heeled shoes. It was her usual escort outfit, her librarian look. 'I'm naked underneath,' she said, if a man questioned the style.

The title of her talk was 'Work in Progress' – she wanted something loose and ambiguous. She had organized her notes around various headings – investments in energy schemes; buying foreign currency; recycling petro-dollars; and spending on leisure. Because she was talking to historians and political scientists she decided to include some basic accounting terms and she began by describing the implied differences between expenses and expenditure, and other misunderstood financial terms. Then she turned to her headings and illustrated each one with a particular person – 'I think the most effective methodology is the case study' – and she made her points by describing various men she had met through the Jasmine Agency: where their money came from, and where it went. She did not mention the agency. How shocked those men would have been! She said, 'In an interview, the subject disclosed –'

'Salim is fifty years old, from Qatar, and has a number of business interests, mainly in oil-related industries. On a recent trip to London he met with an American manufacturer of solar panels and placed orders totalling a half-a-million dollars. These were trans-shipped not to Qatar but to Pakistan, where Salim is developing an agriculture scheme. When interviewed, the subject disclosed –'

When interviewed the subject had been just behind her, furiously bumming her against a mirror. And similar impressions came to her when she discussed 'Mamoun', her foreign currency case-study; and 'Hamid' the film importer; and 'Ahmed' and 'Jabari' and 'Fazal' – the last three were all friends of Karim whom she entertained at Half Moon Street, and whom she suspected of being arms dealers. But she used them to illustrate property and leisure.

General Newhouse, as chairman, summed up her talk by saying, 'This can hardly be called rigorous analysis, but a study of this kind has great charm and subtlety as well as insights. There is considerable merit in this. Questions, please.'

Lauren loved answering questions, and she easily turned

them to her advantage: 'And this reminds me of something else I meant to emphasize –' Her talk was not well-documented – it was not documented at all. But she knew that it was appreciated for being fully human. She had made events and abstractions understandable by describing the men behind them. The men had paid her for her companionship or her sexual performance – but so what? It really was scholarship, of a kind, and later when she was praised she thought: I've earned that.

It was on the afternoon of her successful talk that she received what had become a daily call from Madame Cybele. Somehow, she expected her to say, 'Bulbeck'. She said, 'Karim.' And Karim said, 'There is someone I want you to meet.'

*

He did not at first show her his suitcase. He met Lauren at a pre-arranged spot – the gazebo in the centre of Berkeley Square: she watched the daffodils tremble as she waited – and it was as they were walking together back to Half Moon Street that he produced the metal valise. One minute there was nothing, and the next minute this heavy thing was bumping his leg – certainly heavy, because his arm was straight and tugging his shoulder at a slant. He said his name was Zayid – volunteered it, and so she knew he was lying. People seldom lied to her: what was the point of lying to a stranger? A stranger was one of few people in the world who could be trusted with the truth.

Lauren's successful talk that morning had made her con-

fident and bossy. She took charge and became inquisitive –
Where was he from? What did he do? How long was he
staying in London? He said nothing, which unsettled her –
silence always did – and then when she persisted, for her own
peace of mind, he said, 'I am engaged in various sorts of
business,' and no more.

His English was good: he could have explained. But he
stayed strangely silent – so different from the boasting men
she was used to.

Zayid grinned at the room, at the street, at the pavement
below, at the rooftops. It was a grin of wonder – his smiling
lips and bared teeth expressing incomprehension. Lauren
had seen this grin on the faces of nervous men in hotel rooms
when they faced her. But Zayid was facing the windows.

'Will you have a drink?'

'That will not be necessary at the moment.'

He had the foreigner's pointlessly good English – too many
words. In this way he reminded her of Madame Cybele.

He did not 'require' any food, he did not 'use' cigarettes, he
had a 'very sweet tooth' and where was the 'parlour'? Talking
this way he seemed to be turning aside – Lauren always found
formal English suspiciously evasive. And she could not
understand anyone until the person acted. Because this man
was not saying or doing anything she did not know him. She
had weeks ago stopped looking for motives in men's faces.
She could handle men. After she made them come they were
silly and embarrassed. It was one-sided sex – she got nothing
– but she sometimes maliciously thought of it as castration.
Men were so empty afterwards!

When Zayid took out his camera Lauren relaxed – the

voyeurs were always the silent, reticent ones, just spying on a body, hiding near it and possessing it at a distance, like certain travellers. The voyeurs were harmless. Taking pictures was not sex – that act was a private moment, later, when the pictures were developed: hot hands and bulging eyes.

But Zayid's back was turned. He was pointing his camera out of the window.

Lauren said, 'The Naval and Military Club. They don't let women in. Isn't it awful?'

He did not face her. Had he heard?

She said, 'But then, you probably approve of that.'

Nothing.

She wanted to call Karim and say, 'Hey, where did you dig up this guy?'

He was a small cold man. His grin, which looked like understanding, was incomprehension; his frown, which appeared to be concern, was complete indifference. I can understand sex, and I can understand the fetishism that turns things into sex, she thought; but I can't figure indifference.

She said, 'I've got to make a phone call.'

'No phone calls.'

'Don't say "No phone calls" like that! You're not my father. I want to call Karim.'

'Karim is no longer present in this country,' Zayid said.

'What's that supposed to mean?'

Zayid frowned: he didn't care. 'Ring him if you like.'

She tried – anxiously aware that she was breaking agency rules – but there was no answer.

'He's probably out.'

'He is definitely out.'

It worried her that he seemed to know so much and that he did nothing. He had put his camera away and had stopped pacing the room. He sat down in a chair by the window and went to sleep: was he going to spend the night there?

Lauren did not want to go to bed while he was in the chair. She started doing her stretching exercises, then became self-conscious and stopped. She lay opposite Zayid on the sofa with a pillow under her head, but her interrupted routine – the presence of this man – kept her awake. She did not mind missing dinner, but missing exercise made her restless.

'Where are you going?' Zayid said, without moving in the chair.

'Out. I can't sleep. I'm going to run.'

'Stay where you are,' he said. 'You forget I have paid you.'

Six hundred pounds in a brown envelope – such a thick packet she had had trouble crushing it into one of her shoes in her closet. But she had forgotten the money, because she hadn't done anything to earn it.

She said, 'What do you want me to do?'

'Exactly what I say.'

That worried her and her worry increased when he remained silent for the next three and a half hours, his lids not completely down and his nighthawk eyes shining through crescent slits.

Just before dawn, he said, 'We go.'

She was ready: she had not taken off her tracksuit.

They walked to Berkeley Square down wet yellow-black Curzon Street, passing a policeman and then two gamblers – who else would be just here at this hour? And she was reminded that Zayid had a gambler's wordlessness. At the top end of the square Zayid stopped next to a BMW and he told her to get in.

'I'm always trying to get into the wrong side of the car,' she said, crossing to the passenger side. 'In the States the steering wheel's on the left.'

He said nothing, but his driving put her on her guard: he drove one-handed, too fast, always speeding when the light changed, and turning sharply, trusting to luck that there would be no one crossing the road.

She said, 'I hate these butch cars,' hoping that talk might slow him down.

He sped south, past the Palace and across Westminster Bridge. She watched the signs and looked for something familiar.

'I know someone who lives here,' she said, seeing a sign to Brixton. She was speaking of herself, in that room, in that house, hating London. She could not connect that girl with this woman, the past with the present.

'She's amazing,' Lauren said. 'She makes popcorn and feeds it to the birds. She's real strict about her diet. Like she eats carob? And bean curd? And about a ton of bran a day? She used to be married but she left the guy, because they were always arguing about curtains and whose turn to cook. She started off writing this book about Kissinger, and that got her interested in China. But she's been everywhere. She's always saying that the Chinese have beautiful skin, and Hindus never wear wigs, and Africans have perfect ears and – get this – Arabs never wear second-hand clothes. Jesus, do you have to drive this fast?'

He neither responded nor slowed down.

She said, 'This isn't your car.'

He glanced at her.

She said, 'You weren't driving a car last night when you met me.'

'How do you know that?' he said, surprising her with a full sentence.

'Because if you had come in a car I would have seen it and remembered the licence number. I always do that, just to be on the safe side.'

'What is the number of this car?'

She told him the three letters and the three numbers that she had seen when she had crossed behind the car to the passenger side.

'I knew last night that you were very clever,' he said, and drove faster.

'Clever doesn't mean smart in the States,' she said. 'It means something else.'

He said, 'I mean something else.'

'Where the hell are we going?' she suddenly demanded.

His fast driving was like a reply. They made their way through Surrey, and dawn struck at them – long fragments of light from the end of a long brown set of meadows. She stared at the rising sun until it became a bonfire on those meadows, and it gave the packed clouds in the high sky the texture of smoke. This was old orderly England, looking senile but safe; she preferred this to the trampled edges of London.

'Where are we going?' she asked. She was sorry her voice had a slight tremor of suspicion and fear in it. Perhaps that was the reason he did not bother to reply.

There was no conversation, so she read road signs.

[114]

'Godstone,' she said. 'Piltdown.'

But saying these names into the silence made her uneasy.

'Listen, where are we going?'

He frowned and it meant everything.

Did he know where he was going? Perhaps he was just following any old road in order to speed. She had felt so differently yesterday. *There's someone I want you to meet.* And she had gladly agreed, because her seminar talk was out of the way – little accomplishments like that relaxed her and made her lazy again.

She felt she should deliberately try to make herself feel hopeful.

'I think it's so important to know when to relax. Some people don't know how.'

There were wide hills in the distance with long smooth summits and shadowy hollows, and nothing behind them but great tumbling fume-like clouds.

She said, 'Do you know where you are?'

He snatched at the gear shift and said nothing.

She said, 'I want to go back.'

He ignored her. He looked up each side road that they passed – fifty feet off the main road they narrowed to country lanes.

She said, 'I have to go back. I've got things to do today –'

She had taped her seminar talk. If she got someone to transcribe it and she did a little work on it, she might be able to publish it. She wanted to get that going today and have a good night's sleep to make up for last night.

Zayid turned his face to her, but his eyes were not on her. He was looking past her at a narrow side road, and then he swerved suddenly and aimed the car into it, skidding as he went. Now they were racing down a country lane that was wet black from a recent shower.

She said, 'Unsafe things always look lovely to me, like certain bridges and certain roads, and ice on a lake in the winter.'

She was terrified and could hardly breathe.

'Would you mind slowing down?' Talking helped her get air. She only asked questions when she was afraid.

'Jevington,' she said, as they passed a low black and white village sign. 'Please stop.'

But he swerved again on a yet narrower lane, hardly more than a path, that carried them steeply up a hill into some trees; the curves surprised him, but he did not let up.

She was sure that he had no idea where he was going. He was turning on impulse, looking for the narrowest road, the most hidden place, because – why had she gone when he grunted, 'We go'? – he wanted to harm her. She felt freezing waves of a kind of murderousness coming at her from his body like a strong smell. She thought: He wants to kill me.

He was looking for a place, hurrying towards the end of this empty lane.

She said with useless anger, 'What do you want?'

He stopped the car so quickly she felt a sense of forward movement for a few seconds after he stopped – it was a stomach-sickening weightlessness that was also fear.

He faced her and fumbled in his pocket – for a weapon, she was sure – but she already had the door open and was heaving herself out.

'Stay where you are!'

[116]

'Down from London?'

'No. We were in Brighton. Vacationing and seeing the sights.'

He stared at her, daring her to challenge the lie.

'Eastbourne's much quieter,' the old man said, and the church walls cushioned his words. 'I often go down on a Sunday afternoon if the weather's fine. Planning to be in England long?'

Zayid said, 'That is entirely up to my wife.'

There was something about this obnoxious lie that made her certain that he intended to kill her. The word 'wife' was like a rope around her neck.

'This church goes back to the tenth century,' the old man was saying. He pointed with his umbrella. 'That sculpture in the wall is even older – it was found in a stone chest under the floor of the belfry. It's Christ killing a demon.'

A biscuit-coloured chunk of stone sealed into the wall like a huge tile showed in relief a smooth almost featureless Christ driving a spear into a beast's open mouth.

'That's Saxon. Fifth-century, you could say.'

Zayid grinned at this: his grin was fury and frustration. He walked down the centre aisle, his footsteps ringing on the hard floor. The church smelled of cold paint and waxed wood and damp stone and dangerous roof beams. Hammer beams, the old man was calling them. The bare altar was set in a small enclosure, with an arched entrance.

'Chancel arch,' the man said, hurrying after Zayid, who was grinning at the stained-glass windows. Lauren was backing away. 'See those squints?'

He drew Zayid aside to the narrow openings.

'You'll never guess what they were for.'

Zayid showed his teeth. It was his way of struggling.

'Lepers,' the old man said. 'But they were cut on the slant so that the lepers could see the altar from outside the church. You know what lepers are?'

Zayid's gaze lingered on the old man's tongue, as if the words were still there, and he turned his back on Lauren for the first time while he examined the squints in the arch, saying, 'Leprosy?'

By then Lauren was pushing open the door to the porch and before the door swung shut again she was away, running hard down the lane and through a wet meadow, which was a long hillside at the edge of the Downs. From the top she saw the open sea and at the shoreline in a flat valley the town of Eastbourne – though she did not discover its name until she was well inside it and running towards the station.

*

The train arrived in London just before noon. In the taxi she resolved to pack and go, to leave London at once. Her fear had left her and now she felt a trembly euphoria that she was still alive – lucky!

Out of caution she alighted from the taxi at Stratton Street and walked slowly to Half Moon Street, making sure that no one was watching her. Then she hurried upstairs to her flat. She opened the door and stepping into the room she fought for breath – she steadied herself against the door-jamb so as not to fall.

The flat was empty. It was not robbery – robbery was a sort

of piecemeal plunder, the smash and clutter of things opened and broken. This was something else: it was clean and complete. Everything that had been there was gone – every stick of furniture, every carpet, every picture, every fragment of decoration. Her shoes, her money, her precious coat, all her books. It had been totally emptied, and she was frightened by the nakedness of the place. There was one object – the metal suitcase that Zayid had brought. It was pushed against the wall and in its small solitary way it looked dangerous. The other thing about empty rooms was their obvious stains – the faint trace marks where everything had been.

The bare flat – everything gone – gave the place an absurd nightmare look and convinced her that someone had intended her to be part of this scheme, taken away like all the things she owned: someone wanted to kill her. She felt weak and terrified as if what she was seeing in these hideous empty rooms were symptoms of a fatal illness.

9

Now the flat seemed very dangerous – like a deep unmarked hole – and the cracked bricks on the buildings of Half Moon Street squinted at her in a threatening way as she passed them, hurrying towards Shepherd Market. She had nothing, she was naked under her tracksuit, she was cold without her mink-lined coat. She did not have her briefcase to take to the Institute – not even a pen! But what was the point of going to the Institute? She was finished here, she had been plundered: they had removed everything but her body. It was a fright that convinced her that she was helplessly close to death.

The Jasmine Agency was shut, though she went there anyway to make sure, not knowing whether to barge in and take a chance or to lurk outside. She lurked long enough to find out that it was closed. But it was usually closed in the daytime: the sleazy greedy places and the ugly girls were for the afternoon in this part of Mayfair.

It would have been a relief to her to find Madame Cybele. There was no one else Lauren knew who would offer help. She could not call up anyone and say, 'Help me – I'm in trouble' – no one in that whole city knew her well enough: no one knew her at all or understood both of her lives. To those who knew her as a Fellow at the Institute she would have to explain how she came to be in this situation; so the Institute was out. And all those other men had paid her: there had never been any question of friendship. She had wanted it that way. Friendship was dangerous and cheap.

Karim had put her in this position. She hated him for sending Zayid to her. She wanted to call him and scream, 'You failed – I'm still alive!'

But where was he? Zayid said he was not in the country. And what of Lord Bulbeck? The old secretive man now seemed as suspect and cruel as any other man she had known, and in her fear she began to hate him for everything he had hidden from her.

Men stared at her as she moved through Mayfair wondering what to do next. But only one move was possible: she had to leave. She had little more than thirteen pounds in the shallow pocket of her tracksuit – the change from a purple twenty after buying her train ticket from Eastbourne.

Shepherd Market was full of travel agencies and ticket offices. She chose the agency with the most posters and asked the man at the desk the fare to the United States.

'Which city?'

'Washington,' Lauren said. 'No. New York.'

'Is this first class or economy?'

Lauren pouted and said, 'First class.'

'When would you be travelling?'

'Immediately – today or tomorrow.'

'That would be full fare, I'm afraid. Six hundred pounds, single. Just under, actually. Shall I book it for you?'

Thirteen pounds. Lauren said, 'I'll be back.'

Then she stepped into the street and a harsh voice behind

her said, 'I've been looking all over for you!' And at the same time a strong hand grabbed her roughly by the wrist.

*

Now she was naked on the floor of a darkened room and the man was standing above her and saying, 'You don't sound as if you mean it.'

'I *do* mean it,' she said, in a pleading voice.

'No,' he said. 'You're lying. I don't believe you.'

'Really,' she said, and her voice broke. 'It's true.'

She pushed herself sideways to see his face. He was smiling. He wanted her to beg.

The man was short and had popping eyes and was bald under the nest of hair woven on his head. His penis was a blunt little thing, like a pathetic vegetable tucked under the hairy basket of his belly.

She said, 'I'm dying to take you into my mouth.'

'You're not going to get anything, my girl,' he said, shielding the silly thing with his cupped hand. Then he was encouraged and he caressed it with his stubby fingers.

'Let me do that,' Lauren said. 'I'd love to do that. I want to touch you.'

He said softly, 'You can watch me.'

'Yes,' she said, and now she understood. They were always so evasive! 'Let me watch you' – and moved nearer. 'I love to watch you do that.'

'Do you?' he said, and he repeated it. He was stalling. And he was stiffening – the vegetable had changed colour and now filled his hand.

'That's nice,' she said. But seeing him struggle she wanted to laugh. What a misshapen and ridiculous thing the penis was! Half of them didn't even work properly and all of them looked pathetic and detachable, like some wrinkled sea creature – like something you'd find goggling at you and swaying in an aquarium.

She had not touched this man. He had told her roughly to take her clothes off and to lie down on the floor ('Not on my bed!') and then he pulled the little demanding thing out of his pants and throttled it in his hand. Now he was whimpering as he dripped it on her and all its life was gone.

She said, 'I love that,' and propped herself up so that he could see her face. She was daring him to deny that she was telling the truth. 'More,' she said, and it was like mockery: he was done.

'Don't go,' he said. 'Please.'

'If I stay it'll cost you another hundred' – she was already pulling on her tracksuit.

'Then go,' he said. 'You're a slut.' He was at the door, fumbling with the locks. 'You've got diseases. I wouldn't touch you for anything.'

Lauren knew she had to leave quickly: men could be terrible just afterwards in their humiliation. She had never seen their famous sadness, but only guilt or anger or resentment, or a sullen silence, as they realized they were temporarily castrated – and how did they know at that moment that it was not temporary? No man had ever completely satisfied her, or had touched her as tenderly and deeply as she had touched herself. But she always knew when a man's little frenzy was finished: they came with a pathetic finality – one squirt and

[124]

the rest dribbled and that was all. This dope was still mutter-
ing as he shut the door on her.

Following the signs to the Fire Exit she turned a corner and
saw a man entering a room.

She paused and stared and so surprised him he held the
door open. She said, 'I bet your room has a terrific view.'

'Dynamite,' the man said, after a stutter of trying to find the
word. 'Want to come in?'

'It'll cost you,' she said, and stepped nearer and whispered.
'I'll do anything you want. I just want to please you.' She
implored him and stooped slightly and said in a slavish way,
'Anything.'

The man showed a flicker of hunger and she knew she had
him.

By five-thirty she had turned nine tricks – the term seemed
hugely appropriate. Tricks were what most men wanted. She
had never solicited this way before; it excited her and took the
edge off her fears. The men were eager – she guessed that
they were able to smell other men on her. And most of them,
at last, were glad to see her go – something to do with the
daylight and the street noise and their shame. It was so
different from the night, when they procrastinated and be-
haved like husbands, and whined when she said she had to go.
This afternoon showed her the laughable weakness of men –
how they hurried, how impatient they were, how easily baited,
how willing to pay. She stared, they faltered and fell. They
were looking for her! She had almost twelve hundred pounds.

The good boutiques and chic stores were closed, but
Selfridges was open until eight tonight. She bought shoes,
tights, a handbag, a Burberry and a lovely umbrella, and a silk

[125]

dress. She left her tracksuit in the changing room. Returning to Park Lane she stopped an Arab dressed handsomely in a *thobe* and *besht* as he was entering the Grosvenor House Hotel.

'Yes, please, madam,' he said.

But she had only smiled.

'Can you come with me?' he said.

He brought her to a third-floor suite and a man in a *dish-dasha* opened the door and let Lauren in. He waved the other man away.

An Arab wrapped loosely in a towel lay sprawled on a bed, and the man in the *dish-dasha* returned to him and in a loving way massaged him.

Lauren said, 'I can do that.'

The masseur glared at her, but the man being massaged said, 'Come here.'

She did so, towering over him. He took one of her buttocks in his hand and squeezed it and said, 'I want this one.'

'If you bum me,' she said, 'it's four hundred.'

He said no, but in his eagerness to send the masseur away he miscounted and she got six hundred.

'Stay,' he said afterwards, but she said she was busy – she did not have time for the drink, the dinner, the belly-dancer and the groggy argument at midnight over where she would sleep. She felt enterprising and alive again: she had very little time left. Her goal had been a thousand pounds, but now – even after having bought those things – she had over twelve hundred again and she decided on two thousand pounds even, like a gambler aiming for higher stakes in the middle of a winning streak. She would work all night – she had never stayed up all night before; she would leave in the morning with her money and her first-class ticket. Her tremendous panic was gone. She thought: I've got a hot hand.

She felt powerful – excited and greedy; she felt more willing now to take a risk, having survived what she was now sure had been an attempt on her life. She had nothing to lose; there was no one left to impress. She was indestructible. All she had to do was stay away from Half Moon Street.

She stopped men on Piccadilly. They wanted to be stopped by a pretty girl. She said, 'I'll do anything you want. It'll cost you, but it'll be worth it.' The mention of money made the men eager, for the only thing they had was money.

She sat at the bar of the Hilton and touched the man next to her and said, 'Do you want me?'

He murmured.

She said, 'Lead the way. I'm your wife.'

After midnight the men were louder and rougher. She met them in doorways and they hurried her to their rooms. They had been drinking. The whiners of the afternoon were now asleep; these others were wilder and alcoholic and barely intelligible, but full of insistent and elaborate instructions. One man made her suck him off in the bathroom in front of the full-length mirror; another gave her a vibrator and explicit directions and he photographed her using it on herself; a third had her kneel over a chamberpot and piss while he drunkenly swayed before her and ejaculated against her cheek.

By the time the casinos were closed – three-thirty or four – she had been photographed again – but with her face turned away. She was bruised and had scratches on her arms, and she was saddle-sore from the bummings and the pokings.

[127]

And yet no man had lain between her legs and simply fucked her as Lord Bulbeck had done last week: they were too frightened, too shy, and they were indifferent to her pleasure. Did they know how identical they were in their fears?

She had lost track of the men, of the foolish routines, of the numerous showers that still had not removed that hot oystery smell from her. But in the Ladies' Cloakroom in The Dorchester she counted her money. She had two thousand three hundred and forty-three pounds in cash. She thought: I'm free.

*

There were lights burning upstairs at the Jasmine Agency. She had seen them first in the early hours of the morning as she had passed under the window with another nameless man, and she had thought fondly of Madame Cybele. Lauren's bruises inspired a sort of affection and pity for the woman.

But this ache made her feel slightly diseased, too, and there was something like an illness in the male smell that she could not wash away. The past hours had given her an understanding of Madame Cybele, and she wanted to see her to say goodbye.

She had to say goodbye, because she knew she would never go back; and what she had once regarded as enjoyable, the calculated frolic of a double life that had granted her a kind of power, she now saw as a sickening weakness, a feeble plotting to serve a bad habit.

She hated men now – hated them for being bullies and not

caring about her pleasure. She hated their gross bodies. She hated their smoking and drinking – their decay. Most of all she hated them for not having any secrets. Their real malice lay in being both stupid and strong. They could have anything. They wanted the worst things. She thought fondly of Debbie, and how they had kissed and licked like two cats in front of the video while that man watched them.

The street was empty. She was walking in the direction of the agency. She felt sisterly towards the woman. She wanted to tell her that she understood and she was free. And she had a desire to warn her – to tell her to get away and escape while there was time, as she planned to do herself on this new day. Lauren was out of danger, but this realization made her want to save one other person. It was only fair.

The steep stairs reminded her of her first visit the day after she had seen the videotape – the stranger who knew her well and sent it had never admitted the fact; and then the two Arabs had said, 'We want this one,' and she had been flattered, and she had so easily stepped into this other life.

She took the stairs softly, one at a time, and heard low voices – one was Madame Cybele's, the other was a man's, perhaps Captain Twilley's. She knocked and there was a silence – the darkness of dead air. She listened at the door and knocked again.

She heard a drawer shoved into a desk.

'Come in.'

Madame Cybele was alone, at the secretary's desk, looking up, trying to speak.

Lauren said, 'Why do you look so surprised?'

Madame Cybele struggled to speak and then, unable to

[129]

make any noise, she got up and rushed forward and hugged Lauren so tightly she was on the verge of tipping the tall girl over.

'Hey, what's up –'

'Who is it?' came a complaining voice from the other room – not Twilley.

Madame Cybele said, 'Run!' and Lauren realized that the woman was trying to push her out of the door. But Lauren was having trouble standing. Madame Cybele did not say anything more – did not have time – for in the next instant the speaker from the other room came to see for himself who the visitor was.

'Let go!' he shouted.

Lauren looked up, but she choked when she tried to speak – she was suffocated with fear. She stared at Hugo Van Arkady, who hissed at her in furious surprise.

10

He had taken charge, but he had not said much. He had paused only to gather his raincoat and his wide-brimmed hat and then he had hurried her to Park Lane and hailed a taxi. The streets gleamed – it always seemed to rain in London at this dark hour of the morning. He was giving the driver directions and she was helpless to resist. She was tired and shocked – they had made a fool of her. What affected her most was not the surprise that she had seen Van Arkady in that place, but the humiliation that he had seen her.

Now they were at Victoria in a first-class compartment, with the shades drawn, drinking coffee out of plastic cups. The train was at the platform being loaded with mailbags and bundles of newspapers – every few moments there was a thump or a clang. Lauren faced the gaunt man. Ever since the taxi she had been asking him questions in a trapped and wounded way, but he had hardly spoken and he had not replied to her. Then, unexpectedly, he answered.

'You are catching the ferry to Calais.'

'And you?'

'I'm making sure you catch it.'

'I could have flown,' she said. 'I've got plenty of money.'

'Money!' he said in a pitying way, as if this was the most meaningless thing on earth. He recovered from this word and said, 'They'll be watching the airports. And you don't have much time.'

'Why?'

He shook his head. 'You'll be a great deal safer if you don't know.'

'Where's my stuff?'

'Disposed of.'

'Just like that,' she said.

'Every bit of it is replaceable,' he said with the same pity he had used to mock her with the word money. 'Your worry about it proves how young you are. It was such innocent junk.'

She said angrily, 'And you were going to dispose of me, too!'

'Zayid was supposed to take you away. His plane was leaving from Gatwick yesterday afternoon. That's why you ended up in that part of Sussex –'

So Van Arkady had been listening to her questions and pleadings in the taxi: her story of the car journey and the little flint church near Eastbourne.

'– He might not have killed you. It wasn't in his orders. But these people sometimes use their own initiative. It is cheaper to kill someone – and less trouble, and it's final. Don't say "murder". Simplicity can often seem very savage. This coffee is disgusting.'

'He was a savage.'

Van Arkady considered this. 'Because he didn't make love to you?'

'How do you know that?' But she had the answer as soon as she spoke. 'You bugged my flat, you knew everything, you set me up.'

He said, 'You were our bug,' and seeing Lauren wince, he added, 'You were a live wire.'

[132]

'You and Karim knew all those men.'

'Not very well. We were listening to them, not you. We've never had a bug like you. Education is a wonderful thing.'

'That's why you needed me,' she said.

'Not really. You asked them good questions, but it was more a matter of security. You were one of the few people I trusted – you were completely reliable in your innocence. When I saw you at the General's party I realized you needed us.'

She said, 'You're the person who sent me that tape.'

'I thought it might interest you. You seemed ambitious.' Now he looked at her almost in admiration. 'God, you were busy! You must be very healthy to keep up that pace. But you were also very lucky, you know.'

'I used to think so.'

'Yes. You might have been killed.'

'By one of your slobs.'

'By anyone. Listen, it's dangerous to sleep with everyone.'

'You're a pimp and you say that to me.'

Van Arkady said, 'I hate that word.'

There was a whistle, and the banging of doors, one after another, and shouts. Then there was silence and the train started, without any more sounds. The posters slid by, then a brick embankment, a bridge, a power station, rooftops and backyards looking derelict in the drizzly light.

Van Arkady smiled at the gloom. At lamp-posts a soft brown murk surrounded each saucer shape of light. He said, 'London is an excellent place for murder.'

She followed his gaze and then looked back at him. He was still smiling.

[133]

'It's quiet and peaceful, the police are unarmed, and if you're caught you get a fair trial. There is no torture, no hanging, no firing squad. The sentences are remarkably short and the prisons are clean. Do you know that the best-fed people in Britain are prisoners? Any murderer can study for a degree in sociology. Our people are used to a different sort of justice.'

She said, 'You do mean murder, don't you?'

'Never mind.'

'It was something to do with the flat on Half Moon Street and my name on the lease. What is it, a hiding place?'

He said, 'I hate intelligent people. You can't shut them off. Ignorant people can be nags but they're much more useful.'

She said, 'I know it's Half Moon Street.'

'Your personal effects are gone. You should be glad they are, instead of sitting there pleading for them back. Zayid was just a courier, and you don't know anything.'

'Why did you mention murder just then?' she said, and when he didn't reply she said, 'You're an incredible phony. If those people at the party really knew you, they'd despise you. You're a pimp, you're a sneak, you run an escort agency in order to spy on the poor fuckers you don't trust.'

He said, 'I find you extremely ugly.'

'And you're planning to kill someone.'

He said, 'You worked for us, darling.'

'I could talk,' she said.

'You won't. No one would believe you. And you'll never come to London again.' He gestured out of the window at the last straggling suburbs, the semi-detached houses, the allotments, the black canals. 'If you come back, you'll probably be arrested.'

'I don't have to go back to London to talk.'

He did not hesitate. He said evenly, 'You can still be killed.'

She looked out of the window and saw a woman raising her arms to hang out a blue shirt on a clothes-line, and in the foreground a brick-yard and *Builders' Merchants* behind a rusty fence; she knew at that instant that this was printed on her memory and that she would always see the woman and the brick-yard and the sign and the fence when she remembered *You can still be killed*. Even in themselves they were horribly shabby, but they also signified his threat. These alone were reason enough for her never to come back and be reminded of what this man had said at the very margin of London.

In a small surrendering voice she said, 'How long were you using me?'

'From the first,' he said, and seemed triumphant. 'Didn't you ever suspect?'

'Yes,' she said. 'Periodically.'

He smiled broadly at her and she felt fooled in her lie.

'What if I hadn't moved to Half Moon Street?'

'We would have found someone else. London is full of people like you. The world is. That's why it is so easy for us.'

'What do you mean "us"? Who are you?'

He said, 'The five thousand.'

He did not speak again until they were near Dover. He fixed his eyes on her and his steady gaze seemed to emphasize the distance between them. She had no more questions.

'Don't look so sad,' he said. 'You're safe.'

She thought: But I wanted to save someone else. She

looked away from him, and now they were in a tunnel and her side window had become a mirror. Perhaps the other person I am saving is also me.

*

She did not relax when he was gone, nor when she was on the ferry, for she knew that though she could not see him he was still watching her in his own way. The surface of the Channel moved like a length of cloth in the turning wind. Lauren sat inside with a sad severe look on her face. At Calais the Paris train was enormously waiting at an empty platform. In Paris she bought a green leather suitcase and a cup of yogurt and stayed that night in an American-style hotel. She was exhausted but slept badly, because she was frightened, even here. And what was happening in London?

On the train to Roissy the next day she tried to put the past two days together. She puzzled with them but there was a large piece missing. And yet the rest was vast. There was too much. She thought: It hasn't happened to me yet. She was still trying to make sense of the first terrible day.

At the airport, all the papers on the news-stand, French and English – and every other language – had the same simple picture on the front page. It made a black pattern that ran through the display like a rack of wallpaper or linoleum. She bought *The Times*, *The Sun*, and the London Arabic paper, *Al-Arab* – in this one the picture was repeated larger than in any other paper, which was why she bought it. Here the fallen man not only had a face but an expression – surprise, anguish, and his eyes were whitened with fear. His hand was folded

[136]

crookedly beneath him and great stains soaked his coat.

'Excuse me, miss.'

One shoe was twisted away from his foot, and his narrow elderly ankle was showing. His frailty was obvious in his thin legs and in his brittle posture – he looked as though he had been thrown on those stairs, and broken.

'Are you –?'

But it was this corpse's strange contorted posture that revealed his identity to her. His head and legs set so carelessly gave him an attitude that resembled ecstasy. She had seen him awkward and reckless like that a dozen times, and the last time exactly a week ago all twisted and looking murdered by his passion for her – and right there, too, on Half Moon Street. Horriboo, he would have said. She giggled a little and then began to sob.

'Are you actually reading that paper?'

She shook her head: No – and startled the stranger with her wet eyes and the way she pressed her lips into her mouth in grief. She made an animal motion with her hands – fear – and the man turned sharply away. Was he trying to pretend he hadn't said anything? But even as she watched him go she was still afraid and felt ugly.